MARY RUTH BARNES

LITTLE BIRD

D1566377

A NOVEL

Little Bird

© Copyright 2021 by White Dog Press

ISBN: 978-1-952397-42-4

Book and Cover Design: Corey Fetters

Chickasaw Press
PO Box 1548
Ada, Oklahoma 74821
chickasawpress.com

This book is dedicated to Harry McSwain, my grandfather, who taught me the quiet excitement for life and filled my soul with Chihowa Iowak, God's fire!

TABLE OF CONTENTS

PREFACE

My heroes are those of my First American family. I believe that when we forget our American history, it is because we did not understand those who contributed to it. It is like knowing the plot of the story, but not the characters which bring it to life. The ancestors of my First American family and friends were leaders on which the history of America was built.

This historical novel is based on real people and accounts, particularly the life and love of my great-great-grandmother, Esther McLish. My hope is that you, the reader, take away the knowledge of the many brave men and women who married and loved in Indian Territory. Though they faced many hardships, they found strength among each other, all to make a better life for you and me.

My goal for this book is also to provide a greater understanding of the Dawes Rolls and the painstaking registration process it took for our ancestors to appear on the final rolls. There are many of our First American brothers and sisters that were unable to be placed on the final rolls.

Being declared a tribal citizen on the Dawes Rolls was more than just receiving a roll card number. It meant the ability to receive allotted lands and the assurance that this land would irrevocably belong to us. Our journey would continue on, dreams and visions made possible for future generations of First Americans.

I want to tell you a story about a past—the past and history of my family. I hope for it to become your past and your history, as well.

LITTLE

BIRD

SUMMONED TO COLBERT (1900)

The only way to stay cool on a hot, windless June afternoon was to sit in my rocking chair and fan myself with a paper. My son Holmes napped at my feet, his little hand resting atop my hand-made moccasins. The sun on his brown chest turned his skin golden.

He was handsome like his father, and slender, his long legs curled up against his chest. Scattered memories of my own papa flooded my mind. Smiling, I waved the paper over my little son's sweaty forehead, and I wished deeply that Papa was still alive to see his grandson and to help me be a braver daughter.

I turned the paper over and read the letter from the Commission to the Five Civilized Tribes for what must have been the hundredth time. It looked like an invitation, but I had no choice. If I wanted my son to get a parcel of land that was rightfully his, I had to go.

We would have to start early the next day for Colbert, Indian

Territory, to meet with them. Colbert was fifty miles from where we live in Durwood, and I was a single mother taking a big journey with my son. The trip would certainly be an adventure.

I put down the letter and picked up the newspaper to fan myself. Maybe I felt the stress of thinking about the trip. I wondered how I could explain some things. Some are just unexplainable.

But Papa taught me to always be brave and to face all my struggles with courage and pride.

I tried to get newspapers when I could, to read about what was happening in Indian Territory. I had kept this particular paper for a couple of years. What got my attention most was an article about the president of the United States, Grover Cleveland. I stopped fanning myself and reopened it. The article said President Cleveland told the commissioners they were not being sent to Indian Territory to represent the United States citizens there, but to represent the Indian. He "hoped" that when the Indians were settled, it would be the best for all concerned. The word "hoped" made me chuckle. I was not sure I believed it.

Each time I went to face the Dawes Commission, I felt less assured. My husband's death and the careless Indian census had left my boy without a roll number or an allotment, even though he was Chickasaw, and even though his father died before he was born. But it was only fair for us to stay on our settlement.

Papa would want me to go. My life had not taken me this far only to lose the land that belonged to my last-born child. My families did not come all this way in the Removal for my children to lose their rights to the land given to them in place of the land stripped from them.

The white men wanted to make us all "civilized," but they brought in all the bad people to take away our land and steal our livestock. I knew personally about all of it. It took too many people I loved from me. And the United States itself wanted to take over

Indian Territory. The talk in Tishomingo said the promises to us in the treaties were no good anymore.

Every elder you ran into wanted to discuss the new laws, called "bills," created just to redo Indian Territory. That made no sense to me, calling them "bills." It was in 1896 that a new "Indian Appropriation Bill" came about, with one item in it that struck my attention: the creation of the Dawes Commission. Now I was going to Colbert to face these Dawes commissioners and hoped we would never lose our land again. The whole idea just made me feel plain uncomfortable.

We got up early the next morning and packed our wagon for a trip that would take a day and a half. We would head to Tishomingo for supplies and spend the night with Lavina, the mother of my first husband and the only Nana who Holmes ever knew.

"Get up in the wagon, boy." I smiled at Holmes, who had turned five the previous September. He was a boy of much intellect, like his father. His five older sisters had helped me a great deal to nurture him.

We passed along our fence line and I could see the three old crows moving slowly down the rail, getting ready to take flight. Sometimes they would follow me, and sometimes they just sat on the rail and waited for me to get back home. I used to hate them, but lately they seemed to comfort me, at least now and again.

"Where are we goin', Mama?" Holmes asked, yawning his early morning yawn.

"We are heading to Colbert to meet with the Commission of the Five Civilized Tribes," I told him and clucked at the horses.

"What is a 'civil-died' tribe, Mama?" he asked, stumbling through the words.

"Not 'civil-died,' son. Civilized," I chuckled. "'Civilized' is the white man's word to describe us as being more like them, accepting his laws and ways," I told him. "It's like capturing a wild pony and bringing him back to the yard and teaching him to get along with us."

"I'd like to have a wild pony, Mama," he said. He paused and looked up at me to ask, "But what is a 'co-mis-un'?"

"The commission is a group of men that Mama hopes will help us hold onto the land that rightfully belongs to us," I answered, looking back over my shoulder to see if the crows were following or waiting. "This is going to be a big day for us, Holmes," I explained and scooted a little closer to him. "We are going to Tishomingo today and we'll see Nana Lavina. And then we will go to Colbert tomorrow morning."

Holmes cheered, happy at the thought of seeing his Nana.

After a stop at the mercantile, Holmes and I made it to Lavina's just in time for supper. It was a wonderful visit. Her home was most comfortable and warm. The next morning we got up early for the drive to Colbert.

We got there about lunchtime. My time before the commissioners would be in the afternoon, so we had bread and dried beef in our wagon across the road from the only building in Colbert. It looked like a mercantile store.

I wore my only good church dress, with a solid brown nap and small collar, brown pleated bodice, and a brown skirt. It was the only dress I had that I thought made me look fairly presentable. I overlapped a dark blue apron Lavina gave me because the lace on the border made it look pretty. I put on my good lace-up, brown leather shoes with dark blue socks and tucked the old moccasins Lavina gave me into the wagon for later. I had no reckoning what was going to be asked of me, or what was to happen, but I would put my best foot forward.

I took Holmes's hand and we walked to a bench by the doorway where we were supposed to wait.

A tall, round-bellied man with a mustache from one side of his face to the other came around the corner and addressed me, "Are you Esther McLish?" He reached to shake my hand.

"Chukma, I am, sir. And this is my son, Holmes," I said greeting him in Chickasaw first, out of habit. Holmes stared at his mustache. I nudged him gently, and the man reached to shake his little hand. He kept gawking at the man.

"I am Mr. Green, the court recorder, and I will record what is said today." When the man spoke, his mustache rocked about his face. I looked down so he could not see I was trying to keep the funny tickling at my throat. I had to be respectful and brave. "Chairman Bixby will ask the questions this afternoon, Mrs. McLish. Mr. Bixby is very thorough in looking at the facts of a case. Not to worry, Mrs. McLish. You just answer to the best of your knowledge." He nodded, his tight mouth askew under that big ol' mustache. He walked back around the corner and inside.

I tried not to let my eyes follow him, but they sure wanted to see what lurked around the corner. I took a quick peek and could see a bunch of bearded white men sitting at a big, long table. They all looked right at me, so I quickly put my eyes back on my lap. I shuffled my feet, like I often did when I got really anxious.

Mr. Green called out, "In the matter of the application of Holmes McLish for enrollment as a Chickasaw Indian by blood, would Mrs. Esther McLish step forward to be sworn in?"

I went inside, feeling overwhelmed. I tried to keep my legs from trembling while I led Holmes across the room to where Mr. Green stood. I took a deep breath to calm my nerves, lifted my right hand and put my left on Mr. Green's swearing-in Bible.

Another man placed a bench for Holmes and me. "Yakoke," I thanked him in Chickasaw. All the men sitting behind the desk looked white. I could see other Indians in the room, but I figured I'd be better off talking a language that white men could understand. I think one of the Indians was trying to translate for the commissioners, but I spoke English from there on.

I lifted Holmes to the bench beside me, faced the commissioners, and smiled politely.

A small-framed man in a dark suit came forward and introduced himself as Chairman Bixby. He stood with his hand on his chin. "State your name and age," he ordered.

"My name is Esther McLish and I am forty-six years old," I said, very softly, because already I felt almost out of breath. I knew I wasn't afraid. I somehow just lost a brief moment of confidence.

One of the men at the long table, with a white beard and piercing eyes, barked, "Speak loudly and clearly, please."

I took a deep breath and silently rendered a prayer for courage, asking my Maker to help me be brave and answer with the goodness of spirit I was known to have.

Chairman Bixby nodded, as if to reassure me, and continued his questions. "What is your post office?" he asked.

"Durwood," I answered, louder, of course.

"How long have you lived there?" He began to pace about.

"About eighteen months, this time," I replied.

"How long have you lived in Indian Territory?" He stopped and looked directly at me. His blue eyes were intent on me.

"I have been in Indian Territory, in the Chickasaw Territory, ever since I knew anything. I don't know how long it has been. I was a very small child in the first of the war." I was trying to answer honestly and to not get flustered.

Two commissioners at the table whispered to each other. I thought they seemed a little impolite. I knew my mama taught me better than that.

Mr. Bixby stroked his beard as if he was putting together some thoughts and asked, "Are you a Chickasaw Indian?"

"No, sir. I don't claim to be. I am a Cherokee and Choctaw Indian. I came to the Chickasaw Nation after the first of the war.

My father, Jesse Wilson, was Cherokee, and my mother, Annie, was Choctaw. My papa was a preacher. As far as I can tell, I was never recognized in the Cherokee Nation."

His brow wrinkled a bit, as if he was confused. "Is your name on the Cherokee rolls?"

"Not that I know of. I am pretty sure my papa was on those rolls. He was a preacher."

He continued, "You don't know whether your name is on the roll of 1880 of the Cherokee Nation?"

"No, sir," I answered. I pulled Holmes a little closer so he wouldn't wiggle off the bench.

"Did you ever draw any money from the Cherokee Nation?" he asked, raising his eyebrows a little.

"No, sir, not unless it was drawn by my papa when I was a baby," I replied. I gave in to Holmes and let him sit on the floor, next to my feet.

Then, after only slight hesitation, the man repeated himself, as if he had not understood one word I had just told him. "So far as you know, you never have been recognized as a Cherokee, and your name is not on the Cherokee rolls, and you have never drawn any Cherokee money?"

"No, sir, I have not," I answered. I was starting to feel a little agitated.

He looked down at Holmes and pointed. "What is the name of this boy here?"

"Holmes McLish," I answered clearly. Holmes looked up at me and smiled. I smiled back and tapped him sweetly on his head.

"What was the name of his father?" Mr. Bixby asked.

"Holmes McLish," I answered, still looking at Holmes.

"Was the boy's father Chickasaw?" Mr. Bixby asked.

I looked up at him. "His father was on the tribal rolls."

"Did he draw money as a Chickasaw citizen?" asked another

commissioner behind the big table.

"He did draw his money from the Chickasaw Nation," I answered.

Mr. Bixby asked the next question and wanted to know, of all things, if I was married to Holmes McLish. I could feel an angry flush rise in my face. I assured them all that I had most certainly been married to Holmes.

"Do you have a marriage license and certificate with you?" he asked me.

I did not know I was supposed to bring such a thing. I answered, "Well, I guess the marriage is on record. Hindemon Burris's father, old man Burris at Stonewall, married us."

He asked where we were married and I told him six miles north of Tishomingo.

"Were you married by Indian law or US law?"

"Indian law. I did not carry any license or certificate with me. Albert McKinney was the county clerk and he recorded it. I saw him do it."

Mr. Bixby stepped back to the table and picked up a piece of paper and held it, in some kind of deep thought.

"Why hasn't this boy been enrolled?" he asked.

"They did not enroll him in the census because Mr. Butler was in that neighborhood to take it, but he never came over to my settlement. Most of the time he just stayed at home, and when I went to have him enrolled, they rejected him," I explained in as much detail as I could.

Mr. Bixby stepped closer, never breaking eye contact, and asked, "Do you know why they rejected him?"

All the fear, uncertainty, and endured injustices swirling around inside of me boiled over. In that moment, all the patience and manners I'd prayed for went right out that big, old door, and I blurted, "I don't know why, sir. Just prejudice, I guess!"

"You tried to get him enrolled, did you?" Mr. Bixby asked, unflustered.

"I called his name over, and they said he wasn't on the census roll, and that was the last of it," I answered.

"Was he never put on the roll when he was a baby?" he asked.

"No, sir."

He asked pointedly, "Did your husband not pay any attention to it?"

"I guess not, sir, 'cause my husband was dead," I answered sharply. "He was killed February 20, 1894, and Holmes was born on September 22, 1894."

At that, Mr. Green got up abruptly, walked to the door, and escorted a man into the room whom I recognized as a friend of my late husband, Holmes.

He introduced him as Peter Maytubby and announced he was a Chickasaw commissioner. They quickly swore him in to testify, right in front of me. Mr. Green moved us over next to the wall.

Mr. Bixby began to question Mr. Maytubby. "What is your name?"

"Peter Maytubby."

"Where do you live?"

"I live at Caddo, Choctaw Nation, Blue County."

"You are an official of the Chickasaw Nation at this time?"

"Yes, sir, one of the enrolling commissioners."

Mr. Bixby looked at me, then pointed at us. Mr. Maytubby turned to look, too.

"Do you know this woman, Esther McLish?"

"I have seen her," he said, still looking at me.

"Do you know whether she was married to Holmes McLish?"

"No, sir, I do not," he answered, turning back to face the table.

"Did you know Holmes McLish?"

"Yes, sir."

"Was he a Chickasaw Indian?"

"Yes, sir, recognized as a Chickasaw Indian. We went to school together."

"Do you know whether or not he was ever married?"

"I heard he was married to this woman." Mr. Maytubby pointed at me.

"Do you know whether he had any children?"

"No, sir."

"Do you know this little boy?" Mr. Bixby asked, pointing to Holmes.

"No, sir."

Mr. Bixby thanked Mr. Maytubby for his time and dismissed him. Mr. Bixby nodded for me to come back over. As we walked forward, me holding onto little Holmes's hand, I took a really big, deep breath and rendered another prayer for patience and goodness that my mama and papa taught me. I prayed silently for Papa to take me over and have me to act like he would want me to.

"Did you make application for this boy before the Chickasaw authorities, or did his father?" Mr. Bixby asked with a little softer tone, yet still with conviction.

The man just could not remember what he had asked me. I decided he was just short on his memory, for sure. It definitely seemed to me that this man was used to talking to people who did not give truthful answers, or he was just looking for an excuse to reject every Indian he could. My papa would want me to stay strong. "No, sir," I said and paused to show I meant what I said. "His father was dead." I raised my eyebrows at him, showing him I was smart enough to know he just asked me that same question earlier.

His expression never changed. He asked, "Did you make the application?"

"Yes, sir, I made the application myself."

"So, why didn't they enroll him?" he asked me again.

"I told you a while ago that they did not find his name on the census roll." I was getting myself all upset again. I felt my face flush. And then the question of all questions came at me.

Mr. Bixby, leaning over me with my precious little boy sitting at my feet, asked, "Did you ever hear it claimed that this wasn't McLish's child?"

I reached my hand to touch my boy's head and erupted, "Oh, yes! Lots of them I have heard say so, but I reckon I ought to know. I was his wife. The rest of them wasn't. There is no one else that knew but me, I guess. I was his wife! I ought to know that this child is his! Oh, yes, a whole lot of them has said that it wasn't his, but my dead husband Holmes had another child. He has an older son, and that son has been recognized. Recognized already, by the Chickasaw Nation. They gave all my little boy Holmes's property to that son, named Willie Bourland McLish. That boy is Holmes's and Sis Dufer's child. He was married to Sis before me." I pointed at little Holmes, sitting on the floor next to me, "If you see this big boy and my boy, they look just like brothers. You would know then, for sure."

I realized I had said way too much, but they just allowed me to keep on talking. I was not sure I had done any good at all.

Mr. Bixby appeared not to be upset by my ranting on and on. He asked immediately, "How long did you live with Holmes McLish before he was killed?"

I answered in a softer tone, trying to pull myself together, "We lived together about eight months, sir."

"Who was his first wife?" he asked.

"Her name was Sis Dufer, and then he married one more time before me. Her name was Nancy Lewis. I think she was a white woman, but they were not married very long," I said.

Mr. Bixby wanted to know if any of the other wives were still alive. I told him I thought they were all dead, and that I was told Sis Dufer died when Willie McLish was about six months old. I felt a flush coming over me again. I tried desperately to hold back tears of frustration.

Mr. Bixby told me we were finished with questioning. "We will notify you by letter once your case is decided," he said and pointed toward the door.

I grabbed my boy and steered us both out into the fresh, warm summer air. I took a deep breath, walked to my wagon, and started crying. I felt like a child. I could not stop the tears. Weak and feeling helpless, I lifted Holmes onto the wagon and turned my horses away from Colbert back toward home. I needed to make speed to get back to Tishomingo before nightfall overtook us.

Holmes patted my hand. "It's all right, Mama," he said in his sweet little voice. The tears from my face landed on his little hand.

"I know, son," I said. "I know. It will be all right."

THUNDER'S SPIRITUAL STATE (1861)

It was a sunny afternoon in my seventh year of life in Indian Territory. I stood by the family creek, washing my feet. I knew walking barefoot would make my mama upset, especially if I came home with dirty feet. I watched the water run through my toes and thought how funny it was that my feet were so pink underneath and so brown on top. My skin was dark anyways, but darker now from the summer sun.

I flopped my feet in the water. My paint pony, Thunder, nudged my neck. He hated to be splashed. He pawed at the ground for me to get up. His nostrils flared, like he had caught the true scent of the morning breeze. I pushed his wet nose off me and he turned away to graze.

I prayed to God in Choctaw. "Help me, God, to be a brave and a strong girl someday!" My papa said I had to be brave and he was counting on me. There were some bad men in this territory.

I had to be brave, always.

Papa said many missionaries came to Indian Territory during Removal with the Cherokees, and he learned from them. His faith was strong. He prayed with us and held our hands together, lifting them towards the sky. He prayed for strength and courage in Cherokee. He said this land was ours. He would kiss the earth and let the dirt run through his fingers, touching the soil and calling it his homeland. His heartbeat rang in our ears.

I wiped my feet in the grass, threw my rope over Thunder's neck, and pulled myself up, like I was climbing the side of a tree. The paint pony was small, and even though I was only seven, I had learned to mount him without any help. Earlier in the week I had started with the rope and practiced by tying the rope to the top of the fence rail and pulling myself up the fence post, one foot over the other. After a day of climbing the fence post over and over, I never hesitated again to get on my pony and be ready to go whenever I wanted. It gave me the freedom and independence I craved.

All the same, I also prayed my home would never be taken away from me like it had been from Papa and Mama. They cried about their losses and sang their victories while Rufus, Lottie, and I sat with them by the fire in the long room. Because of their stories, I felt like I took every step with them on the journey of Removal.

Even though I wasn't born when it happened, I could hear the wails and cries like a distant drum. Still, I felt proud. I felt my heart working an inner strength while they shared about the old ways of caring for the earth. I watched and listened while they worried about how they would farm the rocky land. They made plans to get food and maybe some cattle. They told us they hoped we could have a comfortable life. I knew what comfortable meant, like the warmth of a fire on a cold winter day. Their hope became my hope while they revealed their dreams for all of us, a hope that we would have as good a life as Mama and Papa had in their homeland.

"Tell us again about the Mississippi River," Rufus would say.

Rufus was born the same day I was. Mama said I was the oldest because I came first. He did not look like me at all. The story of the roving waters and the waves gave me and Lottie chills, but Rufus loved it. Papa would tell us about the many lives lost crossing the river. But when he spoke of the river, he smiled. He talked of its movement and its beauty, like he would describe his horse.

"The river wrapped my soul," Papa would say. "It gave me strength—a challenge. It was my river of new life." He always said that softly, almost like it was a secret. "The river was like a wolf, moving slowly in and out of turmoil." He uttered a soft sigh, smiled his quiet smile, and said, "And then I arrived and met your mama and her Choctaw family, and I fell in love." He reached for Mama's hand.

I dwelt on those beautiful memories while I felt the cool wind and smelled the early morning smells. I was proud of my native blood, so much that Mama said I could also be a little full of myself. My papa called it God's fire. He would tell me to slow down and breathe.

Thunder became restless. I'd wasted a lot of his "spiritual time" daydreaming on his back, which is what Mama called it when I roamed away on him.

I tossed my hair, my braids glowing in the sunlight. I walked my horse forward, recalling Papa's words, often said in a most authoritative tone. "Get off that pony and walk in the wildflowers, Little Bird. Touch the flowers and feel their petals. They are soft, like feathers. Touch the bark of the trees. Their bark runs in circles, like our lives. The tree grows roots and spreads leaves over the earth. The lines of the bark tell many stories of our ancestors. It is a time for you to remember and enjoy the beauties of God's land. Get off your horse, Little Bird." I would be mesmerized by his words. I looked up to see my three favorite crows on a branch above. They took off, leading the way home. Their feathers glistened in the sun, like my hair.

"Run, run, pony," I urged, realizing my daydreaming was making me late. Mama would be waiting for me to catch her horse for her, my favorite thing to do. We were taking a trip that day.

Ahead of me lay the path to our little farm. The crows chased the sky ahead of me, crisscrossing the path. The water appeared to balance its way down the sides of the rocks—my homeland, my creek, and my rocks. They all made me happy. How could anyone think about living anywhere else?

It was five miles from our house to the closest neighbor, who was sick. Mama was taking Lottie and me to see her. The woman was Chickasaw, and Mama wanted to take her pashofa, which would help her feel better soon. Mama said she was a most-worthy Chickasaw, and I would like their lodging because it was most comfortable. She said the woman's husband was an influential man among the Chickasaws and Choctaws. We found the rest of the woman's family in comfortable health. Mama prayed for us to render unto the Lord for all His benefits. I think she was just being grateful that no one in our family was sick, like that Chickasaw woman was. Mama was always "rendering to the Lord" so she would stay well so she could continue to take good care of us. I was grateful to the Lord that Mama knew how to render.

On the way back, Mama talked about the woman's comfortable house, and a wistful longing overtook her voice and the moment. Then I saw her give me that look, and I knew directly at that moment she was going to check on my soul.

"So, Little Bird. You got up awfully early this morning," she said. "Where did your 'spiritual state' take you? Your papa was worried about you." She flicked her rope to keep her horse moving.

"I rode my horse over to the creek, Mama. I wanted to pick

some paintbrush flowers for Lottie. All the wildflowers are so pretty. You know how Lottie loves all the wildflowers. Thunder kept pawing and was restless, so we stayed there a little bit till he settled down," I explained. I wasn't sure by Mama's look that she was believing my sincerity. I paused and said, with my most charming and sincere affection, "Mama, I was waiting until Thunder's 'spiritual state' improved." I smiled my big-girl smile at her. I knew that was the way she always talked to me, so I tried to look very somber.

Mama and Lottie laughed so hard I thought they were going to fall off the horse. I joined in, not sure she believed me. A beautiful place, indeed, I thought to myself. A beautiful place, indeed.

THE BRAVE HUNTER

Papa wanted us to understand his and Mama's removal from their homelands and how it affected us. I felt like a pebble skipping the top of the water, but wanting to dive deep and learn more. He was a proud man and very proud that his children were born in Indian Territory. He never seemed as angry as others who came to the table to talk. But there was still a pain hidden in his eyes. I knew he tried to hide it. And his optimism about the future for all us kids seemed to bring a bright gleam to his eyes whenever the topic arose.

Once, one of our neighbors came over, a Mr. Richard McLish. He was soft-spoken and a respected leader. He and Papa would sit on the front porch and discuss many things, some of which seemed to have to do with all the guns and unrest around us. He brought his two sons, Richard and Holmes. Holmes was closer to our age, so the boys often came with their papa to play with Rufus and me. Holmes had a way of always wanting to be the boss at everything we played. Richard would stand back and just watch. Rufus and Holmes got along well, but I never really cared for the games they liked to play. I decided it was best that I be polite and courteous. I did love to run and did my best to outrun them all. Holmes seemed really tall for his age, so I would have to really run fast to stay ahead of his long-legged strides.

I overheard Papa talking with Mr. McLish. Sometimes Papa's eyebrows would raise with concern. He would often put his hand on his chin like he had an itch, but I think it was just to help him think a little better. I always liked to listen to find things out, and just maybe I could ask Papa a question after they left. He loved for me to ask questions.

We all ran around the corner of the porch when I saw Mr. McLish stand up. I paused to see what the men were planning next and the boys almost ran over me.

"Are you going to the next council meeting?" I heard Mr. McLish ask Papa.

"Of course," Papa said. "I know the importance of these changing times." He asked Mr. McLish to come inside and visit a little longer. Richard followed his father inside. I told Rufus to grab Holmes and go to the barn to see the horses. I was interested in seeing a little more of this Holmes. I had heard he had a way with horses, and I wanted to see if that was true. He did know a lot about horses. My Thunder really seemed to like him.

Mr. McLish left right before supper, even after Papa invited him to stay. He said he needed to take his boys home before dark for a shooting lesson. He told Papa he should do the same for his children—teach them to shoot. I held onto that thought very closely that evening as we settled by the fire after supper.

I was definitely getting my spiritual state ready to have a good discussion with Papa. I knew Mr. McLish wasn't the only one who liked to come into our yard and talk with him. Our yard was the place to discuss raising stock, trading for horses, and even sharing crops. It was where my papa did his business.

"Why does Mr. McLish think we need to learn to shoot, Papa?" I asked.

"Don't worry, Little Bird. Papa will teach you to shoot soon," he assured me. Papa said he hadn't been worried about our safety until the past July, when he heard about a battle at a place called Honey Springs.

"Where's Honey Springs?" Rufus asked.

"It's north of here, near a town called Muskogee," Papa said as he stirred the fire. "Mr. McLish came here to talk about his concern about the fighting north of us, but I told him we should be safe. It's quite a ways from us. We should be okay here." He sighed, and said, "I will make sure of that." I knew by the way he said it how much he wanted me, Lottie, Rufus and Mama to be safe.

"Last year, the Union army surrounded Tahlequah and captured my friend, John Ross," Papa said. "You remember me telling you about that?" he asked.

We all nodded and talked about many things, like Papa's fond remembrances of Mr. Ross. Mama got Lottie a blanket because she had pulled her bony little knees to her chest and wrapped her arms around them. I think she had been listening a bit too closely to talk about someone being captured.

Papa said he liked to stay close to the Choctaw leaders and missionaries because a lot of his Cherokee friends seemed angry and wanted to get into disagreements. "I want us to get along with all our neighbors," he said. He told us that Mama's Choctaw tribe would be strong in Indian Territory, because like our Chickasaw friends, the McLishes, the Choctaw and Chickasaw wanted peace.

Rufus and I waited until we were old enough to learn to shoot.

When we turned nine, Papa told us it was time.

Lottie was not interested in guns, but Papa knew I would be. He said, "You know I may not always be around you and Rufus and Lottie. You two will need to learn to protect the settlement, if I am not around."

Papa took his long Colt pistol from a high shelf and scurried us out to the field. He was proud of his revolver, which his uncle gave to him when they left Mayhew for Durwood. It had a beautiful wooden handle.

The morning was clear and dry and the air probably a little cooler than a few nights past. Beautiful wildflowers lined the path, looking more alive than the dry earth. I wanted to stop and pick one or two, but Papa was on a mission. We walked a good distance and stopped at a fence made of branches and rope. I could no longer see our home.

Papa lined up six matches, wedged in the fence rail. He shot five matches perfectly, right at the tip of each. I let out a long breath. Rufus and I glanced at each other in amazement.

"Why did you leave the sixth match, Papa?" Rufus asked him.

Silence filled the air. I turned my eyes downward, afraid we were both about to get in trouble for sounding disrespectful.

"There is a very good reason, my children," he said sternly. "There are three lessons in shooting a pistol," he continued, as his brown hand covered my small hand and wrapped it over the handle. He moved me forward, pushing my feet apart. "First, you must know how to be safe with a pistol. Second, you must never miss what you are shooting at. And third, never, never shoot all six bullets. Always leave one bullet in your pistol," he said. I tried over and over, trying to get my aim perfect like Papa's. He said I was a natural, and I felt an unexplainable sense of excitement. My wrist, arm, shoulder, and neck began to ache, but I did not dare complain. I would stay with it as long as my papa told me to.

Still, I was glad when Rufus finally begged to take over.

Rufus screwed up his face and squinted over the barrel. He shot a few times, missed, and got distracted. He liked being busy, and although we were twins, he was taller. We both had broad, fat cheeks, and when he smiled, he looked like his mouth was full of nuts. Papa often teased, "Are you storing food in those cheeks, Rufus?" Rufus would run away, holding his cheeks. Papa would laugh, reach out and grab Rufus, and tell him how much he loved him. My cheeks felt the same as I thought Rufus's looked, but Papa always seemed to look at me with such softness in his eyes. I think he really expected more of Rufus since he was the only boy.

"When are you going to take us hunting, Papa?" Rufus asked. He wanted to shoot something other than just matches.

The next day Papa took us hunting for deer. We sat deep in the thicket, waiting. Papa knelt and pulled me close to him.

"Quiet," he said. "Listen for the deer."

He ignored the first two deer that came along. He let a third pass us by, too. When the fourth appeared, he sat up and took aim. It had large antlers. Rufus and I watched as Papa shot. The deer dropped right to the ground. Papa quietly walked over to the deer and nudged him with his foot. The deer did not move. Papa knelt beside the deer, said some words in Cherokee, then removed the entrails with his knife. He was quick and good at hunting, and we wanted to be just like him.

"Papa, why did you wait until the fourth deer to shoot?" Rufus asked.

"Have I not told you the story of the young boy who became the best hunter in the tribe?" Papa asked.

"No, you have not, Papa. Tell us the story please, please!" Rufus said, as we both begged excitedly.

We sat down by a stream for Papa to clean his knife and his hands, as he told the story of the boy.

"Once there was a boy who wanted to be the best hunter in his village. But each time he shot, he missed the deer. He became very sad and very upset with himself. One day he started to cry because he was so discouraged. He wanted to be a good hunter so his papa would be proud of him. Then he saw something move. It was a very big turtle, walking in the sun. The turtle was hot and tired and did not run away.

"'Why are you walking slowly in the sun, Turtle?' asked the young boy.

"'Because I am hot and old, and I need water. Is there water near here?' The turtle asked the boy and then sighed.

"'Yes,' said the boy. 'It is a way up ahead on this path, where you are resting. It is far, but not too far.'

"'Can you carry me there?' asked the turtle. 'Please, I am so tired and old,' the turtle begged."

"Why does the turtle want the boy to carry him?" Rufus asked, interrupting Papa.

"Let Papa tell the rest of the story!" I scolded my brother. "Please, Papa, finish the story."

Papa continued, with a sternly raised brow, "The boy said to the turtle, 'I will carry you to water, but then I must continue on my hunt for deer.'

"'Oh, if you will carry me to water, I will be so grateful. And I will tell you how to be a good, brave hunter,' said the turtle. 'But you must promise never to hunt me,' he added.

"'I promise,' said the boy. The boy picked up the turtle and carried him down the path.

"When they arrived at the water, the boy sat the turtle down, and the turtle jumped in and dove deep into the middle of the stream, not once but twice, to make sure his dry skin had plenty of water.

"'Turtle! Turtle, you promised to share with me the secret of hunting the deer,' the boy called.

"The turtle said, 'Oh, yes! You were so kind to carry me to water. So, here is what you must do: If the first deer you see is a young doe, you must pass her by and lower your bow to show respect because she will mother many young deer in the future. The second deer you see will be a mother doe with two young fawns beside her. Again, you must lower your bow and walk quietly past. The next deer you see will be a young buck with small antlers. He will father many deer in the future for you and your family. Again, lower your bow, and pass him by.

"'Lastly, you will come to the fourth deer and it will be a big buck with large antlers and many years on him. He is tired and ready to surrender to you. Then, you will raise your bow and kill this big buck. From that moment on, you will be the smartest hunter among your tribe.'

"The young boy thanked the turtle and waved goodbye. All that followed in his hunt for the deer came true as the turtle had told him, and he became a very smart and brave hunter," Papa said.

"That's a great story, Papa!" Rufus said, as he jumped up and pretended to pull back an invisible bow string and aim an arrow at an imaginary buck.

I reached for my father's hand. "I want to be a brave hunter, just like that boy was."

"Then you must always remember what the turtle said," Papa smiled at me, as he pointed to the deer and he stood up.

We walked to the edge of the hill where we left our horses tied and Rufus and I helped Papa lift the deer onto the back of Papa's horse. Rufus was strong like Papa. We rode home east, past Durwood and the Nelda Cemetery. Two men drove by in a wagon and waved at us. Papa told us they were the Fraziers and added that the younger one, named Benjamin, was a nice young man. He must have noticed me looking at him. Papa said they lived north of Tishomingo, near the Blue River. He said the fishing there was good, and he hoped that Benjamin's father, Dixon, would invite him to go fishing soon. He said the water was cold and from a spring and fish out of Blue were good to eat.

I could envision the beautiful Blue River. I felt my heart jump because I had learned so much. I thought I might become a brave hunter someday, and the big Blue River and its beautiful fish would be a sight for us to see. I would have to tell Lottie about it. I hoped the Frazier family would invite us soon.

I turned my pony towards the road home, with Rufus sitting behind me. Thunder never seemed bothered by us riding double. "Double trouble," Papa called us.

It looked like a storm might be coming. I was hoping to see Lottie before I went to sleep and tell her of my wonderful adventure today. I found Lottie wasn't feeling well when we got home. She often stayed home with Mama because she was not as strong as Rufus and me.

Lottie and Mama sat by the fire. Mama was such a beautiful woman. Her cheeks were full like mine, but her skin was lighter than mine and Rufus's. She was slender and as tall as Papa. She was braiding Lottie's hair and they looked so beautiful by the fire. Lottie looked like Papa, but small and frail.

I often heard Mama pray to the Lord that he would make Lottie stronger.

"Mama, we got a deer!" Rufus ran to Mama and Lottie.

"I am so proud of you," Mama said. "We will have good food for the month." She reached her arms out and motioned for me to come join them.

We were a special family and my love of my family was so deep, as deep as the Washita River.

THE TRUTH-TALKERS

The main room in our house was the long room in the back. It was always full of activity in the mornings.

Mama and Lottie were sweeping floors and moving all of us around to get everything clean when Lottie threw her broom to the floor and began jumping over it, back and forth. Mama and Papa laughed.

"What are you doing?" I pushed the broom back at her, trying to make her stop. I grabbed her arm and she started pulling me back and forth, over the broom. Mama sang a beautiful song in Choctaw I had not heard before. Rufus held onto Papa, thinking all the women had drank some new potion that made them go absolutely mad.

"Stop pulling at me," I yelled, jumping with Lottie and feeling silly.

"Someday you girls will 'jump the broom,'" Mama said. "Lottie is oldest, so she is just practicing."

"Jumping the broom? What is that?" I asked, sprawled on the floor, exhausted from all that jumping.

Mama smiled. "Oh, that is what some townsfolk call getting married. I need to teach you girls the old ways of wedding ceremonies. And when you girls decide to get married it will be a hard day for me and your papa," she added with a slight tone of sadness. "In my day, the women were very modest," she said. "We would lay a shawl on the ground for the bride to sit on and hold another shawl over the bride while all the families would bring gifts to her," she said, taking her apron off to demonstrate.

"After the wedding ceremony," she said, "we would have a big celebration with food, and then everyone would dance. The dance was amazing." She swept her apron over us and stomped her moccasins in an up and down motion on the floor.

She told Papa that she and Lottie had seen a wedding in town where the bride jumped over the broom. "Lottie has been wanting to try this ever since."

"Pagan ways," Papa grumbled. Sometimes his religion got in the way of understanding that we were just having fun. He was acting more tired that day than normal. He wiped sweat from his brow, which was odd because it was still cold outside. It was not conceivable to me that he might have been sick.

Mama hurried Rufus and I out to start working the hard soil for planting. It would be difficult to get everything started, but Papa seemed in a particular hurry. Our part of Indian Territory was full of Choctaw and Chickasaw families who supported themselves by ranching and farming the grasslands along the Red and Washita Rivers. Papa said we were poor, but we were able to fit in with our neighbors. We worked hard to till the land, and Papa encouraged hard work, but never pressured us. We just knew it was necessary. Papa made us feel important for helping in the fields. For that reason, we loved helping him.

"Would you and Rufus help with the plowing this morning, Esther?" he asked.

"I will, Papa. I love walking behind the plow. Old Gray is a great horse. She does all the work," I said. Rufus and I ran outside to hook up the plow.

Three crows sat on the rail near the shed. The biggest one scooted back and forth, pecking at the wood, while the others followed him like cows. Rufus lifted his hat to shoo them away.

I grabbed Rufus's arm. "Oh, leave the truth-talkers alone. They aren't bothering anyone."

"What are you talking about, Esther? You have such fool stories," Rufus teased. He dodged when I tried to pelt him with the rope.

"Don't you remember Papa's story about the three crows?" I asked him. "Papa told us if there are three crows following you, they are bringing a truth to you. Two carry the burden of the lie and the third crow, the larger one, is the truth-talker. You are supposed to watch them and be polite. They may bring news you want to hear someday."

"Oh, pshaw," Rufus said. "I don't remember that story, Sis. I think you make up your own stories."

"You just wait until I tell Papa you weren't listening to him about the crows." I was a little perturbed at his attitude.

"Just pokin' fun at you, Sis."

Lottie liked to stay inside and help Mama with the cooking and the inside chores, but Rufus and I loved to be outdoors and working with Papa. There was so much to do on the settlement. Winter had passed and the time to plant was definitely here. He showed us what to do, even though we had watched him so much we already knew. Papa never knew it was more like a game to Rufus and me. We both thought working outside with Papa was more fun than anything we could ever do inside.

Soon, everything was plowed and cleared for the crops to be planted. On the third week of plowing, the sun rose with a bright red hue. It produced a sky replete with tints of white and pink and purple and orange, like a field of wildflowers. Wildflowers were my favorite and I was out early to feed Thunder and Papa's horse, Old Gray. I hoped we would hitch the wagon soon and go into town. The horses snorted and their warm breath made clouds of gray mist around their cold noses. I loved the smell of our horses, and I loved mornings. I wished I could head over to the river this morning, but there was not time today. There was too much work to be done.

Papa, Rufus, and I went into town to pick up supplies and seeds. Papa spent a little bit of time visiting with the general store owner, while Rufus and I carried everything out to the wagon. I noticed that Papa's long Colt was stuffed inside his pants, covered by his shirt. He always took it into town when we went. I asked him once why he did that. He told me it was to protect his family from any harm. I knew the potency of that comment. I knew my papa would protect us with his life.

The weeks flew by quickly, and we planted our grain and vegetables. Papa said the crops would be good that year because he could tell there were hard rains coming. The slight limp on his right leg would hurt him more when the rain came near, and he could smell it in the air. It kept misting that last day of planting, but he knew the rain wouldn't interfere.

The rains came and the crops grew. By May, the crops were plentiful, just as Papa predicted. But we all noticed his weight had dropped while working in the fields that year. Mama filled his plate with lots of food and told him to eat more so to keep up his strength.

Later in May came a day to "reckon with," filled with elements of past and future. Papa had taken to bed more than usual, and one morning sat up with a bad cough. Mama saw blood.

"Lottie! Come here, quick!" Mama called from the back room.

Rufus and I followed on Lottie's heels. Mama stood over Papa, wiping blood from his face.

"I am going to be fine," Papa protested. But he reached for Mama to help him up.

"What is it, Mama?"

"Don't worry, Little Bird," Papa said, and coughed again. "I will be all right." I heard a deep rasp in his voice.

Papa moaned, and Lottie reached for him and told Mama, "Feel of Papa's head. It's hot to touch."

"Lottie, go now and get some cool wet rags," Mama said. "We need to get a doctor here."

"Nah, I will be better in the morning, Annie" Papa retorted, weakly.

"Now, you shush, Jesse. We are not going to let you go on like this being sick. Esther, you and Rufus go get on Thunder and hurry and get help." The urgency in her voice added to my fear.

"Oh, now, it is not necessary for you to get help," Papa said. Then he collapsed back onto the bed.

Mama grabbed my arm. "Esther, you and Rufus go now, and ask Mr. Frazier to go get help from the healer on the other side of the river. And you two come straight back here. Let Mr. Frazier go on his own."

Mama could not go and take all us kids by herself, I knew that. Papa was always too proud to ask for help, and he had told us not to go the other side of the river by ourselves. There were some men there who were not friendly to our kind.

Mama lifted Papa's head, and Lottie handed her a wet rag to put against his forehead.

Rufus and I ran outside and climbed on Thunder, with Rufus in front this time, kicking him to run like the wind. We found Mr. Frazier out in the field with his son. His wife Lavina said she would come stay with us kids and Mama.

It was a very scary day. My head spun and I felt tears coming. But I had to be brave. Papa taught me to be brave. Papa wanted me to be strong.

It seemed like a long time before Mr. Frazier arrived with the healer. Papa held my hand tightly when they came inside. Mama told us all to leave the room and I kissed Papa softly on his hand, my tears falling onto the bedcover. I smoothed the wetness from my face, hoping Papa did not see it.

"Go on, Little Bird, and Papa loves you all. It will be okay," he said, coughing, blood still dripping from his mouth. Rufus pulled me away. My heart was tearing apart. I ran into the long room and knelt on the rug to render the strongest prayer I knew for the healer to make Papa well.

Hours went by. Mrs. Frazier warmed some soup she had brought. Mama stayed with Papa. I thought she was never coming out of the bedroom.

Mr. Frazier stood up and said, "Lavina, I am going to take care of Jesse's animals and then go feed ours. Is there anything you need from the house?"

"Just bring some of that sweet bread for the kids when you come back," Mrs. Frazier said. "Does that sound good?" She turned towards us. Rufus and I nodded to be polite. We did not feel like eating anything.

Just after dark, Mr. Frazier returned and joined us around the fire.

Mama finally came out of the bedroom. She stood by the doorway and said, "Oh, my sweet babies, your papa died."

Her beautiful face was puffy and full from tears. She reached for us. I screamed and dropped to the floor, bringing my hands to my face. I cried while Mama wrapped her arms around us.

I knew I had to cry. Papa would know I had to cry.

32

A SILVER LINING

I looked for days without clouds. The spirit of the sunshine on earth gave me hope after Papa died. The grasses were starting to grow. The earth was changing seasons. Our jobs would be greater after Papa was gone. I would always honor his wishes to care for our land and our family. He would expect no less of me.

Before Papa died he bought a small wagon from Mr. Frazier, so we could take trips into Tishomingo. I was not one to wear a dress often, but Mama wanted me to look more like a girl when we went there. She always called it our "Sunday best," even if it wasn't Sunday. At eleven I began to look more and more like her. My body was changing without my consent and my emotions were strong. Sometimes Mama said my feelings were "worn on my sleeve." I thought that was a silly thing to say. I was not ready to admit I was approaching womanhood. The loss of Papa created a new family strength, but none of us were sure we wanted to grow up so quickly.

When we went to town, we would see important people getting ready to go into the big council meetings. They were called legislators and they met several times a year. We had a governor instead of a chief. When I saw men going into meetings, I would always think of my papa. He loved to meet and counsel with the elders and would be so proud to see the progress. We saw the Fraziers in town and Mama spoke with them.

The next day, Mama gathered us up to go check on Mr. Frazier's wife, Lavina, who had not been feeling well when we saw them in town. It was the polite thing to do. We found her in comfortable health and getting around much better. Mama had an unrelenting allegiance to the Fraziers for helping us when Papa died.

I went out into the yard to visit with Benjamin. He was a little older than me, and handsome, and seemed to like to talk with me. We visited about the weather, and he asked about my horse. Thunder did not particularly like other people, but since he pulled the wagon for us, I was interested in showing him off.

"You like riding Thunder?" he asked with a kindly look and a side grimace.

I wasn't sure if he was trying to make fun of me or if he really wanted an answer. Thunder blew steam out of his nostrils. I think Benjamin was enjoying the moment with him.

The three crows sat on the fence nearby. One kept cawing and interrupting us. *I don't like it when these three crows keep following me and Mama*, I thought. I saw one on the porch right before Papa died, and now I had three making noise at me. I guess Benjamin saw my expression.

"You don't like the 'secret-givers,'" he observed, rubbing my horse's nose.

"I like the crows," I said, "but they seem to always come around in the fall, and when someone is dying."

Mama called me to bring the wagon to the porch. I was really enjoying talking with Benjamin. He kicked at a rock on the ground, which made me think he felt embarrassed or awkward. My brother Rufus sometimes did that.

"Good to see you, Little Foshi," he said, calling me by my nickname in Chickasaw. I smiled and waved goodbye.

Mama and Lottie laughed on the way home, teasing me that Benjamin liked me, and talking about how he called me the name my papa gave me. I said I thought he called me 'Little Foshi' because he forgot my name was Esther.

"You know, someday my children will all move away from me, when you marry and have children of your own," Mama said.

"I'm not leaving you, Mama, and I am never getting married," I insisted.

Mama said we were beautiful young girls, or at least that was what she thought. "You girls turn heads when people see you coming, you are so beautiful," she said. "And of course, Rufus is so handsome."

We laughed. Mama said we would probably marry by the time we were fourteen or fifteen and move to our own homes, but I was not ready for that yet. I knew Rufus was already interested in a girl two yards over, but there was too much work to do for me to consider thinking of things like that. And I did not want Rufus going off and leaving all the work for Lottie and me.

"Benjamin just likes Thunder," I admitted, sheepishly.

They laughed again and we snuggled to keep warm in the wagon. The temperature was dropping and clouds billowed over the red sky. I loved the red skies in Indian Territory.

Another wagon passed us on the road and Mama waved.

"Chukma," we all greeted the new family.

"That was a new Chickasaw family moving in," Mama said.

I saw three children in the back of their wagon. One was a girl who might have been close to my age. I felt it was time to meet new people and learn more. Papa would want that. He always took me with him when he met new people. He taught me the quiet excitement for life and his nature was to enkindle love and kindness among everyone he met. I wanted to follow in his footsteps. I just wanted to be a good person, like him.

Rufus wanted me to get up early the next day before chores and hunt deer because we were getting a little low on meat, but I was tired from the journey and chores of the day before. We had built a corral on poles to hold the horses, but we let the cattle run free, and they came up in the evening to feed. Still, Mama worried about letting them run free with all the new families moving in.

"You need to keep an eye on our cows," she reminded us.

"We will," I said, "but why are you so worried?"

"There are people coming in by railroads now." She sounded concerned. "They may want to take our cattle and our lands."

"Where did you hear that, Mama?" Rufus asked.

"There was talk in town after the council meeting," she said. "The government made promises to us, but the talk is that the white men are still trying to get our lands." She wiped a tear.

"Mama, please don't cry. Rufus, Lottie, and I will protect our lands, I promise." I hugged her tightly.

Rufus declared formally, "Esther, I fear this is happening despite all the promises of protection and peace made to us in every treaty and despite agreements that were made by both sides in the Reconstruction Treaties."

"Well, how did you get so smart?" I asked, surprised.

"I heard the elders talking, too," he replied. "There was talk of separation of tribes."

"Oh, Mama, does that mean we will have to move?" I almost panicked.

"I will not move," Lottie pouted. "I refuse to move."

Mama took us in her arms that afternoon and rendered many

prayers for us. She assured us our lives would be full, and we would all be just fine.

I went out early to feed the horses and check on the cows. As I came around the side of the corral, I saw the crows on the fence, waiting for me.

"What do you want with me?" I yelled at the biggest crow. I stared straight into his eyes. His blackness glistened with iridescence in the morning light. I wanted to swing my bucket at him. He sat calmly, then cawed loudly over and over, as if angry with me. I sighed and apologized. "I'm sorry. I respect you, but I need you to stop bothering me at my work," I lifted feed up to the horses. I wanted to be polite and not offend the "bearers of truth."

The two smaller crows took flight. The third hesitated, looked at me one last time, and followed them.

Mama would have thought I was crazy for talking to the crows. Maybe that's why Papa called me Little Bird—I was a crazy bird talker. "Ha," I laughed out loud at myself as I carried a grain bucket out to the field and watched our cows come over the ridge of the hill to be fed. They were all here. Today was a day to be thankful.

I heard a sound from the other side of the barn. "Who's there?" I yelled.

It was Rufus, walking in on Papa's horse, which I guessed was now his. A big buck lay across his horse's back. He pulled the antlers up for me to see. "You see, Little Bird, I can hunt just fine without you," he boasted. "This will give us lots of meat."

"You are a good hunter, Rufus. Just maybe not quite as good as me." I said, laughing.

"Look at his antlers, Little Bird," he protested. "This deer is far better than any I have ever seen you come home with."

"You are right," I said, admiring the buck. "This one will surely give us lots of meat for the rest of the winter. Papa would be proud if he were here. Mama is going to be really proud." I helped him take the deer down and went inside to tell Mama, before returning to help Rufus skin and prepare the meat. He pulled and removed the hide, and I cleaned and hung it out to dry. He wrapped the meat and placed it in the ground under the shade so it could stay cool. The meat would be chewier and dry this way, but good for us.

I went inside to clean up while Rufus cleaned some of the bones and was not in the house long when I heard hoofbeats in our yard. I reached for Papa's long Colt and went to the door, opening it just enough to peek through. There was Benjamin, with a goofy grin on his face.

"Chukma, Little Bird."

"You scared me to death, Benjamin Frazier," I said. I was delighted to see him. "What are you doing here?" I let him inside.

"My mama made some fresh bread and sent me over to deliver it." He handed me the warm bread wrapped in a cloth. "And I thought you might want to go down to the river—you and Rufus, I mean—and do some fishing. My mama needs me to catch some fish. You wanna go?"

I turned to Mama, who flashed me a peculiar smile and surprised me by saying, "You go, Esther. We need some fish. Rufus should stay and finish cleaning the deer bones." She took the bread and gave me my coat. "Kucha kapussa! It's cold out."

"But, Mama, Mama, I need to stay and help Rufus." I stumbled over my words.

"Now, Esther, you go on and catch some fish," she said, still with that curious grin. "Besides, Thunder needs some 'spiritual time' with you." I could hear her chuckle.

So, off I went into the cool, sunlit day. I gathered up my horse and rode up beside a man who I thought should be at least nineteen years old. It was like I was in a dream, riding above the soil and the earth, floating on my horse, light as a feather. I kept looking over at Benjamin. He was so handsome, but quiet.

"So, you really love to fish?" I asked.

"My papa and I love to fish. I saw you fishing once with your papa," he said.

"So, you were spying on me?" I teased and galloped ahead.

"Slow down, Little Bird," he yelled and hurried to catch up.

I was glad for our time together. He did love to fish. I am not sure why this moment seemed special, but it did. It was like Benjamin knew I was in mourning for my papa. He seemed to be genuinely interested in talking to me. I was just past being a child, although I never acted like one, anyway. It was again a time of change, a time when I was growing up, and a time to be "reckoned with."

While we rested our horses at the riverbank, the place I often would dream about, I found myself constantly glancing at him. He, of course, would turn and look at me. Sometimes our eyes would meet, and my whole body would shiver.

Even though we fished several feet apart, I felt his gaze. His silence kept me guessing what he was thinking. I knew our friendship could be more than special. I was feeling his presence in my heart, which was beating so hard I was afraid he might hear it.

We had several fish to bring home. The three crows swooped before us as we rode back from the river that brisk afternoon. I said nothing of my fear of the message the crows might be carrying. It was a day I would ignore the crows completely. There was no time to be bothered with them.

THE COURTSHIP

We became close to Benjamin and his parents, Lavina and Dixon, who were like second parents to me. Mama relied on Lavina's friendship, and Rufus felt the loss of a father figure. Dixon filled those shoes well.

One day, Mama came home from a visit with Lavina. "Well, the Fraziers are packing to move," she told us sadly. She set her basket on the table.

"Oh, no!" I reached for my boots.

"Where are you going, child?" she asked.

"I need to go say goodbye to Benjamin—I mean, the Fraziers!" I rushed out.

Mama followed me, saying, "Now, don't stay too long. They have lots of work to do!"

I jumped on my horse and headed at a solid run to their place, where Benjamin was packing up one of two wagons. I pulled the reins.

"Whoa, there, Little Bird," Benjamin said, putting up his hands to slow my horse. "Why are you riding like the wind?"

"I—I heard you were packing to leave," I blurted. My face felt flushed. I tried to hold back tears. I shook my head and blew out a breath to keep from crying.

"Yes, Little Bird," he said. His endearing look raised goosebumps.

I was hurt and mad, but the way he looked at me changed me so quickly. I did think he should have told me sooner about them leaving. I swallowed my anger and smiled. "I came to say goodbye to you and your family," I said, dropping my head and sliding off Thunder. I did not want him to see me so emotional. I handed him the reins. He tied up my horse, reached out for my hand, and held it as we walked inside to see Lavina. It felt so natural, he and I walking together, hand and hand. She saw I was upset and offered me a chair.

"Esther, your mama was just here," she said. "I so enjoy her visits and will surely miss them. What brings you here in such a dither? Did Benjamin not tell you we were moving?"

"Well, I was going to, I—I just didn't know what to say," he stammered.

"No, ma'am, he did not." I raised an eyebrow and cast a frown at him.

She told me they were going to move near their relatives and cousins.

All I could think about was how much I was going to miss them.

Benjamin walked me out to my horse. He locked his hands together to make a step to give me a leg up. Then he stopped, unlocked them, and reached up to brush my cheek.

"I cannot imagine my life without you, Little Bird," he said tenderly, and the shivers came all over me again. He cupped my cheek softly with his hand, and I looked deep into his gentle, kind eyes. They were bright and beautiful and made me feel safe and warm inside.

And then he did something I never experienced before. He took his hand and lightly touched my hair and then reached in towards my face and gently kissed my lips.

I jumped back in disbelief, into Thunder, who whinnied his objections. Benjamin chuckled.

"What was that, Benjamin Frazier?" I blustered. I touched my lips and looked back into his deep brown eyes. Then I did something crazy—I had been known to act crazy. I reached up and kissed him back. He pulled me close. I could feel his heartbeat—or was it my heart? I remembered it fluttering the day Benjamin and I first went fishing together. It was something I did not want to stop feeling. I pushed my way out of his arms and jumped onto Thunder, riding out at a dead run, I don't know how far, or for how long. I couldn't breathe. Tears ran down my face. What was I feeling, and how could I let Benjamin leave me? It was a terrible thing to ride away like that, but I did not want him to go, and I had not cried like this since Papa died. I could barely see where I was going. I rode so fast I ended up a half of a mile past our entrance.

When I got back home, I saw Benjamin standing on the front step with Mama. I guess they were looking for me. I wiped my face and slid off my horse, exhausted.

Benjamin rushed to grab my hand and pull me toward Mama. I dragged Thunder with one hand, and he dragged me with the other. I'm sure Thunder thought we had both gone mad.

"Mrs. Wilson, I have not asked Little Bird yet, because I want to ask you first," he said with a determination I'd not heard before. "I'd like to ask Little Bird to marry me, with your blessing, of course."

"What?" I said in disbelief. Right then I recognized in Benjamin's face the love I was feeling for him. It was such a wonderful, mutual feeling.

"Be quiet, for once in your life, Little Bird, and let your mama answer me." He took Thunder's reins.

Mama smiled broadly. "Why, Benjamin Frazier, I would be honored to have you as a son-in-law. But first, Esther must decide if she will have you."

With that he dropped to his knees and took my hands. "Little Bird, I, ah—I mean, Esther Wilson, will you marry me?" he asked. Thunder began to chew the back of his hair. He put the horse's rope in Mama's hands.

"Yes!" I jumped into his arms and knocked him to the ground. We lay there, laughing.

Mama offered us a hand up. "Will one of you please go put Thunder in the corral?" She hugged us both. Benjamin and I turned to hug my horse. We all laughed with joy.

What had started out as such a sad day became the most beautiful day of my life. The sadness returned when I realized I would be going with the Frazier family to the Blue River and be moving away from Mama, Rufus, and Lottie and her husband Jim. I did not like change, but I was happy to have found the love of my life.

So, at the age of fourteen, I was married to Benjamin Frazier. Benjamin was only nineteen, but the age difference seemed huge to me at times. We were married by Judge Jegle of the Chickasaw Nation. Benjamin's friends, Cubby Love and Kyle Smith, were present at our wedding, along with their wives. The move to the Fraziers' family settlement was grand, but I felt an enormous loss because I had to leave Thunder. The Frazier family owned so many horses, and Mama needed him. It was a tough decision, but the right thing to do.

Tribal leaders worked out of Tishomingo, now the capital of the Chickasaw Nation, and we lived nearby. Many Chickasaws and Choctaws were becoming successful ranchers and farmers. My hopes were high that Benjamin and I would be successful, too, in our new life together.

THE BLUE RIVER

The cold, rushing water poured through the jagged limestone on the far side of the river, spewing mist like ghostly spirits with clouds of dampness that clung to Benjamin and me while we fished in early morning. It was his favorite spot on the Blue River, Papa's favorite river to fish, running a hundred miles across Indian Territory.

We enjoyed the same things and his family helped us build a home and make a good living raising cattle. Lavina was like a second mother to me, a beautiful woman with a deep-inside-her-soul kind of beautiful. Her hair glistened with just a light shade of gray, but she did not look that old. She was delicate and refined. My mama thought a lot of her.

Several months into our marriage I had begun to feel sick. I thought at first that I had acquired a flu or ate something spoiled, but Benjamin never seemed sick. I tried to keep my morning sickness quiet, not knowing at first what was going on with my body.

We had now been married almost five months. I told Lavina of my morning illness.

"You are most likely pregnant with child," Lavina exclaimed. "I hope so! I will be so excited to be a grandmother," she continued. "Your morning sickness should get better soon."

I didn't tell Benjamin, just yet. I had not felt sick the morning we went to the Blue to fish. I did step about cautiously, and he took my hand while we walked along the rocks into the cool stream to look for fish. I carried a small spear I made from a bois d'arc branch and used it for balance.

"I am lucky, Little Bird, that I found you." Benjamin said. We kissed and held each other tenderly. "You make my life good, because you want to go with me wherever I go," he said. Then he speared his first fish of the day. "See, I am lucky, and today I am lucky at fishing." He smiled and caught me because I slipped and almost fell into the water. He was tall and slender, much taller than Papa. He looked like most Chickasaw men, with rounded cheeks like me, but oh, he was so handsome. His face was brave-looking and strong, like my papa's face.

"Ha! I thought I found *you*, Old Man?" I teased. He did not like me calling him that in front of others. "You are going to be a real old man, soon," I said. "You are going to be a father."

"What?" he looked startled and jumped a little. "Ah— how—how do you know? Are you sure?" he stammered. He kissed my cheek.

"Yes, I am sure," I said. "Your mother talked with me and explained why she is sure I am pregnant. I was having morning sickness."

The day was spent looking for and catching fish. Benjamin was shocked at how good I was at it. "Aba Binili is with us today," he shouted, holding a speared fish to the sky.

Our home was most comfortable. The Fraziers always had enough food and clothing and were kind, giving, and loving people. Lavina was going to make a wonderful grandmother, or "iposi."

The winter went well and so did my pregnancy, after the first three months. The delivery of our daughter was an easy one. Lavina was with me to help during my labor. She told me the position of the baby was good and that I was a strong, young woman so I should have an easy birth. Lavina covered me in blankets and held my hand.

"Where is Benjamin?" I asked, feeling a little panic because he was not in the room.

"Don't worry, my dear, he is just outside. I will bring him in as soon as we bring this child into the world."

Not many cries and moans came from me. I tried to be brave in front of Lavina. Finally, after several pushes, our daughter was born. Her wails brought Benjamin bolting through the bedroom door to my bedside. Lavina handed our daughter to him to hold. Seeing our daughter in his arms, brought a sudden rush of emotions and tears of joy, flooding our bedroom with the beauty of life. We named our little girl Jessie, after my papa. She was such a tiny baby. He would have been proud.

A week after Jessie was born, we decided maybe she had come earlier than she was supposed to, because she had some breathing difficulties. Benjamin went to the alikchi, who gave him some herbs to burn near her crib. They smelled of pine needles and cedar.

When she turned three weeks old, she worsened. Benjamin went to Tishomingo to ask the alikchi to come look at her. He returned with the white man's doctor.

"Who is this white man?" I whispered nervously.

He took me aside, lowering his voice. "The alikchi was over to Fort Washita and would not be back until next week. This doctor was already in town seeing people and I asked him to come. It will be okay." He took my hand.

The doctor was from Ardmore and came to Tishomingo once a month to see patients. He gave us some medicine and asked me to try to get her to eat more. I nursed Jessie, but she did not gain much weight. We spent many a restless night taking turns propping her up to help her breathe. I lost weight trying to care for her. One night in May, when she was three months old, she got worse.

"Not to worry, Esther." Benjamin kissed my forehead and then little Jessie. "Pack some things and we will take her to Tishomingo. I am going to get Mama. She will go with us and find Jessie a doctor."

I rendered a prayer as we got ready, and it was near dark when we left. I rode in the back of the wagon, Jessie in my arms, while Lavina and Benjamin shared the front seat. I hated the back of a wagon. It reminded me of when they carried Papa off for his burial. I tried hard to shake the memory.

By the time we got to the doctor it was very late. Jessie's lips were starting to turn blue.

I started crying. I could feel my heart falling into my stomach like a big rock, and my chest hurt at the thought of my little baby girl suffering. I kissed her blue lips and rendered another prayer. The doctor worked with Jessie all night, but she passed away early the next morning.

I cried and screamed, "No, no, please, Lord, do not take our Jessie from us." Benjamin wrapped his arms around me, sobbing. I shivered in painful sorrow. Lavina wrapped her arms around us all. I held Jessie in my arms watching her sweet eyes and face fade from us. "Oh, why is this happening to us?" I cried out loud.

Benjamin took our sweet little baby girl from me and kissed her all over her face. He said, "I love you, Jessie," and kissed our daughter goodbye. We held each other and cried out loud again together. We had lost our three-month-old baby girl. No one should ever feel the pain we felt that night.

After Jessie was buried, I became very sick. Lavina came to help, and Benjamin asked her to stay a while and care for me. I stayed in my bed for almost a month with sadness of loss. I never again felt a loss like that. It was different from losing my papa. It was like a part of me died with Jessie. I doubled up in bed like a little baby, hugging the blankets and praying so hard for my baby girl to come back to me. I missed her so much. I could feel her skin against mine. I cried into her blanket.

At the end of the fourth week, I dreamed about Papa. He stood at the end of the bed in a long white shirt and looked like an angel. The glow of the lantern flickered behind him. He told me I needed to get well for Benjamin. I woke up with my face and hair wet with my tears.

That morning I got up and got dressed. It was time I started doing my part around the house. I started cooking and cleaning house.

"What are you doing, Little Bird?" Benjamin asked.

"It is time for me to be about my business as your wife, Old Man," I said. "I have mourned my daughter long enough." I reached for his hand. He smiled and nodded softly. I could see clearly the love in his eyes.

"I am glad you are feeling better, Little Bird," he said and kissed my lips. We had not kissed in several weeks. It felt good to have his face touch mine. It felt more than good to have his skin close to me once again. "Now, you must eat and get your strength back," he said, touching my hair, running his fingertips over my forehead. He hugged me, filling me with a deep assurance of his love.

I knew he mourned with me. More than once over the past month I had looked out to see him at the stream behind our home, crying out to the heavens for our baby girl. I never told him I saw him in the depths of his grief.

I rendered a prayer that God would give us another daughter one day.

The summer heat was hard on me. The weight I lost was not easy to gain back. I was trying to eat normally, but my hunger was not the same. Lavina sent food several times a week, thinking I probably wasn't cooking. I was, but not with the joy I once had in it. Benjamin and I were close, but I could still see his pain and I know he could still see mine. I prayed that time would heal our sorrow while we worked closer to home as winter came near.

Lavina brought over a letter from my mama. I started to read it, but then put it away. I know Mama was sad she never got to see or meet Jessie, so it made me sad to read it. I was happy to learn my sister Lottie was having a baby.

Lavina had promised to visit to catch up on our quilting. We had worked on quilts very little since Jessie passed. "Are you up for quilting today?" she asked, walking through my front door.

"Yes, I am. Spending time with you would be most pleasant." I offered her the rocking chair Benjamin's father made for me. "I am so sorry I lost your granddaughter." I touched her hand. My face flushed. I feared I would break down again.

A small tear came into her eye. She told me, most assuringly, that she loved our Jessie so, but Benjamin and I would have other beautiful children. She spent all afternoon comforting me. I needed her so much that day. "If I know my daughter-in-law, she will give me many, many grandchildren." She smiled and looked down at her quilting. "You know, I had two miscarriages before I had Benjamin," she said.

"I never knew that."

"I don't talk of it much," she said. "But if you go to our little cemetery by the river, you will see two small crosses with both my girls' names on them. I lost two daughters, one right after the other. I know this is so hard for you, Esther, but you will get through this. And the day will come that you and Benjamin will have other children."

At that moment, Benjamin came through the doorway from his chores. "What are my two most beautiful women doing today?" Benjamin said as he walked over and kissed his mama on the forehead.

"What about me?" I pouted.

"Oh, Little Bird, you know I love you," he said warmly. He kissed my forehead, too. He reached for his rifle near the door.

"Your lunch is packed on the table," I told him, wondering what he planned to do.

"Where are you going, son?" Lavina asked.

"I am off to Boggy Depot. Watch after my girl today, Mama. I probably won't be back until into the night."

Lavina looked concerned. "What in the world for?"

"I am going to meet with a man about some new cattle up from Texas," he said.

I hated for him to make the trip alone. It was getting dark earlier, Boggy Depot was a long drive by wagon, and I worried for Benjamin to travel there. The place was full of cattle traders, stores, and a blacksmith shop. It was where the Butterfield Stagecoach delivered our mail, but I also heard of robberies and shootings there. Still, I knew Benjamin was counting on getting a few nice head of cattle to add to our stock. Papa always told me trade was good at Boggy Depot. I never wanted to deny what I was told by my elders. It was my belief that those before me knew much more than I knew.

Lavina and I worked all day on the quilt, a beautiful design she created, and I enjoyed our day of laughter and tears. I took the material to her settlement a short walk away and wanted to get back home to clean up and start a meal for Benjamin.

I saw the three crows on the corral gate. I really did not want to see them and hoped I had left them behind in Durwood. I had begun to dread the truths they might bring to me.

I lit the lantern, put some wood in the stove, and saw the letter from Mama on the table beside the lantern. I thought if I finished reading it, it might help get my mind off missing Benjamin. I cooked our supper and put the plates on the table, covered with cloths. I picked up the letter, sat in the rocker, and pulled a quilt over my legs.

My dearest Esther,

I think of you daily. Lottie moved out and into Jim Tuskatubby's place. She is pregnant and will have a child soon. She is still not as strong as I wished she was. Keep her in your prayers, Little Bird. You are sorely missed and loved with all our hearts. We are doing well and are comfortable. Rufus is also happy with his new bride, Mary Cordelia, and they are a dear sweet couple. We call her Dealie. She is a beautiful girl and so tiny. I hope you can meet her soon.

I heard from some of Papa's people up near Mayhew and Tahlequah. They wrote of all the troubles with some of Papa's cousins in Arkansas. Smallpox struck them while they were encamped at Bentonville in February and March. The white soldiers, for the most part, escaped the disease, having been previously vaccinated. Most of the Cherokees there, however, had not had that advantage and many died before the doctors could check the spread of the disease by vaccination. A smallpox hospital was set up to keep the people who were sick separate, and try to stop the disease, but it will be spring before this disease gets any better. I have rendered a prayer for our family there. I more than expect you to do the same.

I am so sorry to hear of the loss of your little baby girl Jessie. Papa would have been so proud of you knowing in his soul that you named your child after him. You will have many more daughters, Esther. You are not to fret or make yourself uncomfortable over this. I wish I was there to just hold you and hug you and tell you with time, the pain will get easier. Your memories will never fade, but your pain will fade. I pray for that.

    My always faithful love,
     Mama

I thought of those poor Cherokee people and their illness and knew their condition was the most pitiable imaginable. I took to my knees to render a prayer for Papa's family in Arkansas. I prayed for Lottie and her new husband, and for her to stay strong and healthy. I continued in prayer for my dear husband and his safe trip home to the Frazier settlement, and to my arms. My heart ached in missing him. I wiped tears from my eyes as I thought of all the love I had for my Benjamin and the daughter we lost.

I awoke in the rocker. I went out to the porch and saw no sign of the wagon. It was getting so late. Maybe, I thought, he ran into more deals on cattle and decided to stay over and drive home in the morning. I put our cold dinner away and went to bed. My ears strained to hear the wagon. I rendered a prayer for his safety, once again.

I awoke with a start just before daylight, but there was still no sign of Benjamin. I walked into the long room to light a fire, thinking I needed to go out and check on some of our stock, but knowing most likely Benjamin's father had done that already. I was so worried I couldn't think clearly.

THE WAGON

By noon there still was no sign of Benjamin. I rode over to Dixon and Lavina's to ask for their help. I took a long-sleeve shirt of Benjamin's for warmth and brought it to my face, breathing deeply the scent of his skin on the fabric. I thought of his hand-some face and his strong determination to always be there for me. I should have gone with him. He would have probably refused, but the word "no" usually did not go very far with me. I rushed out, his shirt around my shoulders.

I grabbed a rope and whistled for my horse, named Blue, after the river. He was actually black with a bluish shine, which made me think of those stupid crows. I hoped they were not out there. But as I neared the corral, the biggest one sat on the fence post, cawing his nasty rhetoric at me again.

"Go away, fala," I shouted, calling them by their Chickasaw name. "I am in no mood for your cawing today."

The crow bobbed his head like he spat out a seed, but all that came out of his mouth was more hateful cawing.

"I wish you would leave me alone."

He ruffled his feathers, paced up and down the fence, and took off. I pulled up on Blue and kicked at him. I was anxious to get to the Frazier settlement. I saw the other two crows pick up flight behind the first.

I drew close to the bend in the road, heard a wagon coming, and prayed it would be Benjamin. But it was Dixon.

"Is Benjamin back?" he called as he pulled his wagon up. "He was going to come over this morning and help me cut wood."

"No, D-Pa," I answered. I called him "D-Pa" because I could not call him Papa. "I thought maybe I should head to Boggy Depot and see if he broke down or something. That wagon was not the best of them." I tried to hide the fear in my voice.

He agreed and followed me back to the corral to leave my horse. "Why don't you stay here? I can have Lavina come sit with you."

I had no intention of staying behind. I had already waited too long. I scrambled up onto the wagon seat without looking at him, and fixed my eyes on the horizon. "No, let's go. Benjamin needs us."

He studied me a moment, then clucked to the horse. We rode in silence a while.

"Where could he be, D-Pa?" I asked, to move away from the thoughts whirling in my head.

"Not much tellin'," he said. "Like you said, that wagon of yours is pretty old. Maybe he had a problem with one of the wheels, and decided to get it fixed before headin' back home."

In mid-afternoon we spied a man on horseback. D-Pa greeted him and asked if he had seen any other wagons on the road. He replied he had seen one about three miles back, pulled off with a broken wheel, but did not see anyone in or near it. The way he described it, we were both fairly sure it was Benjamin's.

I rendered a silent prayer. D-Pa moved quickly down the road, until we pulled up in front of Benjamin's wagon. I could see the front wheel laying part-way down the hill on some rocks. The wagon had been headed back home on the high side of the Blue River, and looked like it lost the wheel after it hit a boulder, perhaps in the dark. I jumped out and yelled for Benjamin, D-Pa behind me.

I found Benjamin lying about halfway down the embankment, and scrambled down. He lay motionless, his clothes wet from the water running over the rocks around him. I pulled him close and touched his face.

His head had hit the rocks and was caked with blood. I cradled him in my lap and moaned, tears streaming down my cheeks. The grief was so deep, I couldn't breathe. D-Pa wrapped his arms around his son and me, and we cried as we held the limp body of the one we loved so. We knew he was gone, but all that mattered was that we loved him and wanted him back. I am not sure how long we cried, but dark was coming. D-Pa at last stood and gently pulled me up.

I looked up at him in the moon-painted darkness, seeing his wet tears on his tired face. I used my apron to wipe them, and went to get a quilt from under the wagon seat. When I returned, D-Pa held my hand a few seconds before we carried Benjamin up to the wagon.

My thoughts pained me at having another loved one wrapped in a quilt in the back of a wagon. I climbed in beside Benjamin's lifeless body in the back of the wagon. D-Pa did not argue with me about riding back there.

He carried me into my home. I felt so broken in my heart.

He brought Benjamin in to lay on the bed beside me. "Esther, I will be back shortly. I will go get Lavina to help clean up Benjamin and prepare him for burial."

After he left, I crawled out of my bed and I dropped down to my knees.

"Why? Oh, why, Aba Binili, do you take everything I love from me?" I wailed with such anguish. I had cried so many tears there was nothing left of me. The loss of a child and a husband in the same year was more than I could bear. I reached my hands to the heavens and wailed like a warrior. My life felt empty and so hollow at this point, but Papa raised me to be brave. There had to be more for me to do in this life.

I saw the four corners of my shelter—the north, south, east and west—and knew my journey must take me in a different direction, that I had to move past this, and move on. I lay my head across my folded arms. I must have fallen asleep for a few minutes, or maybe I passed out on the floor.

My dream took me into a fire flaming with color. I saw to the north a big, white horse rearing in the wind, with the flames at his tail. I saw to the east a big, yellow pony, running with sunlight hitting his mane. To the south, a black stallion raised his head above me, earth and dust kicking at his heels. To the west was a beautiful red pony, running away from me and the fire. I awoke, my face damp with tears. I had still been crying even while I slept. Why I dreamed of the four directions represented by wild horses, I am not sure. Was it to force me to choose a direction for my life? The dream was vivid, and I felt lost trying to understand what it meant.

I rendered a prayer my mama taught me. "Oh, Aba Binili, give me the answer. Tell me what to do with my life, with nothing left in it."

The world under my feet seemed no more real than the world of the dream I had. The door opened and Lavina stood with the radiance of the rising sun shimmering around her, as if she was an angel sent by Aba Binili. She ran to me and held me, long and hard. She was not my mother, but was the mother of the man I loved and lost, and the mother of a son she lost and loved. And, like me, she was now childless.

"Hold me, Lavina," I sobbed. Life had become more fragile than I ever thought it could be.

She went for a bowl of water to wash my hands and face before turning to her son Benjamin to begin cleaning the blood from his forehead.

I knew I had moved far beyond my emotional age of sixteen. I felt like an older woman, lost in my tragedy. "Please stop for just a minute, Lavina, and hold me," I begged. "Oh, please, just hold me, Lavina!"

We cried deeply in each other's arms.

THE TRIALS (1902)

I was called back to Ardmore in late October and early November of 1902 to be questioned. They said they were bringing in some other people to speak on my behalf. In all my wildest dreams, I would have never believed that I would have to continue to battle for my what was rightfully ours, for so long. I knew Papa would be proud of me.

"Where are we going today?" Holmes asked me.

"We are heading back to Ardmore, Holmes. Mama has to talk with the commission again." I tucked a blanket around his legs. My daughter, Ella, and her son Harry climbed in the back. I was glad they were coming with me. It seemed to get colder as we got closer to Ardmore. I hoped that day's questioning would not be as long as past times.

I was sworn in again. The examiner for the commission was not Mr. Bixby, and the man recording was a Mr. Rosewinkle. He swore me in and put me on that same bench. I sat Holmes on the floor beside me, because it was just easier that way. I realized, looking over the group of bearded men, that they were the same ones I saw two years ago. I guessed they traveled all around. I wondered if they remembered the people they questioned. They all still looked very official. They called me forward, and I stood.

I, Esther McLish, began to be interrogated.

One man looked at me. I felt a cold chill in my bones and tried not to shake. He did not change expression. He asked, his voice sounding ancient, "What is your name?"

I said my name was Esther McLish.

He asked how old I was. I told them I was born in 1855.

The commissioner said, "You are forty-seven?"

I said "Yes, sir," realizing he truly thought I was dumb and could not add my years up.

"How long have you lived in the Chickasaw Nation?" he asked.

I told him I had lived there for as long as I could remember. He wanted to know if I was born there. I told him I was born in the Choctaw Nation. He wanted to know my father's name, to which I answered him, "My papa's name was Jesse Wilson, and he was Cherokee," most politely, even though he already knew it from the papers in front of him.

"Was he a Cherokee Indian by blood?" he asked.

I answered again with a "Yes, sir."

And then the questioning turned for the worse. The commissioner asked, "He was not a freedman?"

"No, sir," I said.

"He was a Cherokee Indian?" he asked again. I firmly believed all these commissioner men needed to get their hearing tested, because he had asked me that same question just two seconds before. These men didn't even look like they were related, but they sure had the same hearing problem from somewhere. I hoped it wasn't in the water.

"Yes, sir, he was full-blood Cherokee, and came over the great big Mississippi River to get here from the homelands," I replied.

"Do you claim the rights of a Cherokee citizen?" he asked.

"No, sir, because I was never there. I was born in the Choctaw Nation, somewhere between Mayhew and Fort Smith," I replied.

One of the helpers came over and offered me a chair. I was glad, because my dress was not comfortable. I had already tugged at my sleeve once. I thanked him and sat quietly down, wishing it had some leather or softness to it. It was hard, like the room. I wished I was in my old rocker at home.

The man questioned me again. "You are an applicant for enrollment of your minor child, Holmes McLish?"

I said, "Yes, sir."

I folded my hands in my lap, and hoped they'd think I looked more comfortable. I was not. I could feel it was going to be a long, long day. I thought if they had just come by the settlement when we were all there, they would have known these children were mine, and they can sure tell we are Indian by looking at us.

"How old is this child, Holmes McLish?"

"He was eight years old the twenty-second of September," I answered.

Little Holmes stood up and waved at the judges, and I quickly motioned for him to sit back down. Ella moved to keep her little brother quiet. I tried not to sigh or show any signs of distress while the repetitive questions continued. It was not polite to do otherwise.

Besides, I knew the wrath of the Lord might come down upon me if I showed any signs of disrespect. My mama taught me better. I respected them—I did—but I think I was just plain scared at this point. Scared I would say the wrong thing. Scared I would mess up. Scared for both of us. I knew if I messed up Holmes would not get his rightful allotment and we might not have a place to call our own.

"The man who was murdered, this Holmes McLish, was he Chickasaw?"

Again, I said politely, "Yes, sir. A citizen by blood of the Chickasaw Nation."

"So, the only rights you make claim to now is as an intermarried Chickasaw?" he asked.

And I said, "Yes, sir."

The commissioner asked, "You have been married to a citizen by blood of the Chickasaw Nation?"

"Yes, sir. All four of my husbands were citizens of the Chickasaw Nation."

"What was the name of your first husband?" asked the commissioner.

"His name was Benjamin Frazier and I married him about two or three miles below Tishomingo. Cubby Love was the county clerk then and I married Mr. Frazier at his house in 1869."

"When did you marry Holmes McLish?" the commissioner asked.

"In 1893, and we were married by Hindemon Burris's father, old man Burris," I said.

"How long did you live with him?" he asked.

"I lived with him about eight months, until he died," I replied.

"Have you married since his death?" a second commissioner interrupted to ask me.

"No, sir. I have never married again since Holmes McLish died," I said and pulled little Holmes up to the bench with me.

"You lived in the Chickasaw Nation all this time?" he asked.

"Yes, sir," I said.

As if that wasn't enough information, they started with the same question again.

I wondered if they had records of my questioning before, because they were asking me the same questions as they had two years ago. Either they were trying to see if I would say all the same things, or they really did not have my last information, at all.

The second commissioner asked me, "You say, that marriage was in ninety-three?"

I said, "Yes, sir."

The questioning then turned to find out how long Holmes and I lived together and I said it was eight months, or nearly, I guessed. "May my children step outside?" I asked. I did not want this type of questioning to upset Ella or little Holmes.

"Yes, they may," the commissioner agreed. Ella took Holmes's and Harry's hands and walked out.

Next, the man with the ancient voice came at me again, with the same questions, again. I began to think to myself that this man must be at the loss of his ears, because Papa told me that if you lose your ears, you will repeat things. He did just that.

Looking straight at me, he asked, "You say you were married to Holmes McLish in ninety-three?"

I said again, "Yes, sir."

And then he scratched the top of his head, as if the loss of his ears had now gone to his scalp, and said, "What was the date of that marriage?"

I must have been so flustered and plumb out of my head myself, because I responded I didn't know the date. Now, any fool would know the date of their marriage, since I'd just said it earlier. I am certain it no longer mattered whether the man could hear me or not, because I just really disrespected myself at that moment. Then he persisted, as if my lack of knowledge and disremembering would no longer matter to him, and wanted to know if it was the first or the latter part of the year. Coming to what little senses I had left at this point, I softly whispered, "It was in the spring of that year, sir." Someone on the other end of the big table asked me to speak up, so I repeated it a little louder.

I moved my feet on the floor, my boots making a soft, scratching noise. I took a long breath, in and out. I thought I'd better relax, or they would fluster me again. I knew little Holmes was getting tired. Ella sat outside the commissioner's room, trying to entertain him, while I sat inside, trying to be the woman Papa raised me to be.

I could hear voices outside. I guessed I was not the only one wanting them to get on with this register. The Dawes Commission was flooded with people trying to get these roll numbers. I told one of my neighbors that the first list they made was not good enough. They were missing people left and right out of where I lived. I did not know why, but I know they missed our neighbors. Maybe because they were out plowing in their fields. People can't just sit on their front porch and wait for people to come count us as Indians.

I kind of jumped in my seat when one of the taller gentlemen rose quickly to walk to the side of the room. At first, I thought he was coming around that big long table right at me and it startled me. He looked down at a piece of long paper laying at the end of that big, stout table and walked back to his chair. He was gray in the hair, obviously some kind of elder. He asked how long I had lived with Holmes McLish. I told him it was about eight months and I had lived with Holmes until he died. "Holmes was killed in February 1894," I said, as I tried to compose myself a little better.

The elderly man introduced himself as R.L. Murray, and wanted to know if my husband Holmes died the year after I married him. He seemed well-spoken and a very educated man, but I knew they were talking in circles and repeating themselves. I had never seen the like of this. I knew these men had to be educated, but they sure didn't act like it. He asked me if my child Holmes

66

McLish was born in 1894, on the twenty-second of September. I reached down in my pocket for my kerchief and wiped my brow.

I told him, "Yes, sir, that is when my little Holmes was born," and that Holmes and I lived together the whole time we were married until he died. I told Mr. Murray that Holmes was from out west, close to Reck. Most of my husband's family was from around Ardmore, but he ran his cattle in Reck, further west. I told the man I did not want to go or live there, although Holmes would go out there and stay a while, and come back to where we lived, and that I was at home when he was killed.

I remembered that my papa built a fear in me about the west. He told me it was wild, and that I was never to live there. Holmes told me there was a Comanche reservation near Reck, and Papa had told me the Comanches were not friendly. Once, Holmes had a run-in with a Comanche trespassing on his land. I did not tell Commissioner Murray all that, but I felt I should have. I just kept it to myself. But I could feel that Mr. Murray acted as if Holmes and I were separated, somehow. I knew we were not, and I knew it was my fault I never went with him. But Holmes was a good man, and he understood. I was feeling a little upset, and tried to keep from crying from all that pushing at me with crazy questions.

I said, looking straight at Mr. Murray, "Holmes owned cattle he ran at Reck and he went out there to check on his cattle. Everyone we knew understood that is what my Holmes did. I never went with him to Reck. It was my own fear that kept me from going there." I explained it as politely as I could. I tried to be more settled in my talk.

Mr. Murray seemed a little flustered at me for a minute. He asked, "Is it a fact that you and Holmes McLish were separated at the time he was killed?"

I raised my shoulders up, feeling such frustration. "No, sir. We were only separated when he would go to Reck, but he always wrote to me if he was going to be gone awhile. We loved each other."

He huffed, a frustrated sigh, and pointed a finger at me. "Then you were not living as man and wife the day he was killed?" He raised his voice. I hoped my children could not hear this man.

I pushed my dress down, sat up straight and said very politely, "Yes, sir, we were living as man and wife." I wiped my face with my handkerchief.

"Do you have evidence that you were married to these Chickasaw men?" the first commissioner asked, referencing my previous marriages.

"I haven't got them here. I can get evidence, I guess. For the biggest part of them, I guess I can," I responded. I had a feeling they weren't sure I could. I wasn't positive myself that I could find the evidence needed, but I was sure going to give it my best effort.

The commissioners all stood and said it was time to take a break, and they would be back after they ate something. I was not even hungry. My appetite was all "ate up" by that Mr. Murray. I almost wished Mr. Bixby was back asking me questions, instead.

I walked out of the courthouse and saw my kids over by our wagon. I hugged Holmes. The air was fresh and cool, and I could breathe again. I was so grateful Ella and Harry came with us, because I did not think I could have made this trip alone, like I did two years before.

We climbed into the back to eat. Doing that brought back memories of my childhood, but the back of the wagon was not a place of joy for me. It only reminded me of death and tragedy.

A CHANCE RENEWED (1870)

A little more than a week after we buried Benjamin, I awoke one morning knowing my life would never be the same. I needed to go outside. I walked down below our settlement to the rocks on the edge of the inexhaustible Blue River that ran down the hill and through my life. I sat at the bottom of the hill, out of sight of the home I helped Benjamin build. I saw the spring water flowing over the rocks, balancing its way down like water falling down the sides of a pail. It poured deep into the edges of the rocks, and bubbled up into a foam. He loved those beautiful rocks. I didn't know if I wanted to ever look at them again. All I could see was my Benjamin lying on the rock where Dixon and I found him. I could not get the sight out of my mind.

I skipped a few pebbles across the river into the shadows of the rocks. Little red ferns burst like wildflowers out of crevices. Some trees were only new sprigs, like lone warriors rising to face their enemies. I wanted to shed a few tears, but the only thing that came to my eyes was the beauty of this place and the aching question, *What am I going to do now?*

I started thinking about where I might go if I left this place that held so many wonderful and tragic memories. I thought about Tishomingo, where new businesses were coming in. I thought maybe it was time to move back to Durwood and help Mama. I missed Rufus. Lottie was mother to a little girl, and I was anxious to see them. I missed Thunder. I told myself to wait a week or so, then I would tell Dixon and Lavina I was moving back to Durwood.

Benjamin's funeral was hard, but it was good knowing he was buried near the Blue River, the place he loved and where he lost his life. I felt confused that day, but the one thing I was sure of was my decision to move back home, near the Washita River. Mama told me she would always welcome me back.

As I rode my horse over to the Frazier settlement, I heard a caw behind me. I looked back, and there were the three crows, circling like buzzards, following me. It was an uneasy time for me, but I had to be brave. I knew I must get my life together. I had to ignore those crows. I kept moving forward and did not look back again.

The Fraziers greeted me with love and concern, and made it hard to settle into a quiet moment. I carefully moved them into a conversation about my life and what I should do. They took the news well, and understood my decision. Lavina would always be like a second mother to me, and I was sad that we could not give her a grandchild. I resolved that if I ever married again and had children, Lavina would be included in our lives. I loved them both so, and was grateful for their acceptance of my decision. They offered me great comfort and rendered many prayers for me.

Dixon had repaired the wagon and found the wheel would have made it if Benjamin had not hit that big rock in the dark. I knew he had been trying to get home to me when he died and thinking about him again made me choke up. I tried to keep my mind on other things. I bade my farewells and drove the wagon home to pack.

I got to Tishomingo just before dusk and decided I'd better spend the night. There was a family Dixon knew, and I stopped to see if they could put me up. Mr. and Mrs. James Brown welcomed me. Their son, Houston, was a constable for the Chickasaw Nation in Tishomingo. They put me in a room with a small bed next to his little sister, Minnie Brown. The twelve-year-old was very talkative and active for a child, and I fell asleep listening to her chatter. I felt embarrassed the next morning when I awoke and realized my failure to stay up with her. She was asleep, so I quietly removed myself and went out to hook up the wagon.

Houston was feeding the animals, and greeted me politely. "Mrs. Frazier," he said. "We are so sad for the loss of your husband in such a tragic accident." He removed his hat and laid it to his chest.

I looked around for just a second, to see who he was talking to, before I realized it was me. I had never been called Mrs. Frazier before, but I guessed that was because Benjamin and I had really never left the settlement. I'd always thought of Lavina as the only Mrs. Frazier I knew.

"Thank you, kindly, Mr. Brown—to you and your parents for your hospitality." Trying to be courteous, I quickly added, "I do apologize for the intrusion into your home, but I was not sure I should be traveling after dark."

He started to say, in Chickasaw, "Yakoke," by which I knew he meant, "You're welcome," but hesitated and went back to English.

I laughed and told him I was familiar with both Chickasaw and Choctaw. I added that I was sorry I could not stay awake for very long last night while his sister talked me into a pleasant slumber.

He made a quiet, soft chuckle, bringing his hat back up to

his head. He was a tall young man, probably close to my age. He was in posture like a statue. I started feeling uncomfortable and turned to my wagon. "We call her 'the one who talks a lot' in Chickasaw." We laughed. It was my first laughter in a week. But I was ready to get on the road.

He helped me mount the wagon and touched the wheel to look at the repair. I am not sure why that gesture brought the image of Benjamin back to me, but I burst into tears. I turned away hoping to hide them, knowing full well I could not.

"I am sorry, Mrs. Frazier. Did I do something wrong?" he asked.

"No, you did not, Mr. Brown. I should be the one apologizing to you." I explained that I probably should have left the wagon behind since it was the one in the accident with my late husband, but I was not sure how I would get to Durwood otherwise. I am not sure why I bothered to give him an explanation, but I delivered it quickly. I composed myself and took the reins. "Yakoke, Mr. Brown," as I clucked to my horse. *What was wrong with me? I am stronger than this.* Papa had taught me to be strong. I saw Mr. Brown wave. The place and time were not at fault. It was all the mysterious things that brought my life to a tragic state. I felt troubled, but I knew there were many who loved me, and that I had to be brave.

By the time midday passed I had come to Durwood. I hoped to find Mama and my sister working on the land. I turned the path down to the yard and saw Thunder in a pen, prancing and snorting. His long, black mane glistened in the light, and his nostrils flared steam in the cold air. He whinnied, a long, low sound, and I saw Mama look up, a rope in her hand. She came running with open arms. I could see she knew, as I stopped the wagon and jumped down to greet her. We held each other in a strong embrace.

THE INNER FIRE

More people were moving into Durwood Settlement. I saw new strength among Chickasaw and Choctaw families. After two weeks with my family, I began to feel my place again with them. I spent many days riding and running errands for Mama into Tishomingo. My horses, Blue and Thunder, became good friends, and I loved the town that Tishomingo was becoming.

Tishomingo was called Good Spring in the early days because several springs flowed into Pennington Creek. It made a good stopping point when traveling from Fort Washita to Fort Arbuckle, and had become the capital of the Chickasaw Nation. Although the Chickasaw population was small, they lived well, and were driven for success. I did not travel much to the east to Boggy Depot, and never west past Durwood. Mama and I went to church in Tishomingo, and often visited the Browns. Houston came out to visit me once at our settlement, but usually I ran into him in town whenever Mama and I went to shop for supplies, or to church.

I admired how Mama had made it on her own, never remarrying. She was a beautiful woman, but the lines in her face made her look and seem much older.

Rufus lived with his wife, Dealie, on the settlement beside us, acquired through a generous gift from the Fraziers. He enjoyed hunting, and was always supplying us with wild turkey or a prairie chicken or two. He also loved to fish, and at times I would go fishing with him.

I decided one day to head into Tishomingo with Mama and my sister to pick up supplies and to look in on the quarterly meeting of Choctaws and Chickasaws. I'd heard Houston was going to speak about issues pertaining to cattle thievery, and I wanted to hear what he had to say. Women were not allowed to sit with the elders, but I could listen from the back.

"Mama, do you want me to hook up Blue to the wagon, and I can ride in behind you on Thunder?" I asked. She agreed, knowing I might want to stay longer.

The meeting was rather long, and Mama and Lottie left before it was over. Houston introduced another constable from Milburn, a white man named James Meredith Raper, who was also a minister. They talked about the cattle rustling going on east of Tishomingo, and said it was going on in places where white men were trying to claim parts of Indian Territory. The constables and elders wanted to go to Washington to ask for help, and tried to pick who might go. I saw Houston look my way and blushed. I turned and headed out to the Mercantile.

As I came out of the Mercantile with some cloth to make a dress for Rufus's new baby, I ran into Houston, his hat to his chest. "Good afternoon, Mrs. Frazier. Did you enjoy the quarterly meeting?" he asked.

"Why, yes, I did, Mr. Houston Brown. It was quite informative,"

I am not sure why, but I spoke in a whisper.

"If you would, please, Mrs. Frazier, speak up a little. And please, just call me Houston." He smiled.

"If I am to do so, then you must call me Esther." I smiled back, raising my voice a little. It was not like we did not already know each other.

"I will, then, Esther." He reached to help me off the boardwalk. "As not to bother you, as I see you are leaving, but I was wondering if I might come out to your settlement some day, and spend the afternoon visiting with you and your family."

When he came before, he spent most of his time talking with Mama. I thought I should remind him of that, but an instinct told me not to mention it. "I am not sure what official business you would have out our way, Mr. B—ah, I mean, Houston," I answered with a bit of a grimace at my slip.

"Oh, Esther, it is not official business, at all," he explained with a slight smile. "I am hoping to get to know you better, as I have not had the opportunity to meet or visit with such an inquisitive young woman. Many women care nothing about our meetings, but I see you carry a great interest in the affairs of our Nation and our people."

"Well, Houston, that is very observant of you, and yes, I am very interested in learning more about our council." I said, edging toward my horse. "My papa taught me to be very aware of the growth of our Indian people and the direction we were taking. He was often in meetings of his own to determine the best for our family. That is why he moved us to Durwood."

"It sounds like your papa was a very smart man."

"Yakoke," I thanked him for the compliment. "I will be home the rest of the week, so please feel free to ride out to our settlement." I remembered my chores and added, "It is best you come for the afternoon." I stepped past him, trying not to look excited about him coming out to visit me because, truthfully, I wasn't excited, at all.

My life at seventeen was fragile. I had just lost the two closest loves of my life. The life ahead was uncertain and many signs told me this new land and new place had much to offer. I wanted to move slowly.

I want to be with Mama and my family, I thought, while that handsome man stood there, looking at me.

"Your papa sounds like a man I would have wanted to know," he said, and reached to help me up on my horse, but I was already on. He looked a little embarrassed, as if to realize that I wished to get away from him. He stepped back. I nodded a farewell and clicked to Thunder to take me home. I never turned to look back at him. I only saw the path home and, just maybe, a feeling of youth coming back to me. I let it be a portent of good things to come. I had to think ahead, and of myself. I could not look back. The pain would overcome me again. As Papa used to always say, "Look at what is around you, Little Bird," and "take time to feel and smell what is right in front of you."

"That is what I am doing, Papa. That is what I am doing," I said to the sky.

Halfway home, I looked behind and saw the three crows making swoops along the path, as if they wanted me to hurry. They made me uneasy. I tried to find a place in my head between instinct and reason. I kicked Thunder to pick up the pace.

As I came into the settlement, Mama, Lottie, and Mollie ran toward me, waving their arms. "Ride over to Rufus's, and check on him," Mama shouted. "Please hurry, Esther!"

"What's wrong?"

"One of their horses just came running into the yard, like something scared it. I thought I heard shots towards Rufus and Dealie's place."

I spun my horse towards Rufus's settlement and kicked hard. I felt sick. I always had known when something happened to Rufus. Whenever he fell and hurt his knee while we were children, my knee hurt for a week. I didn't feel anything, so I believed he must have been okay. Still, I rode like the wind.

I saw him on the front porch, holding his Colt revolver and my stomach dropped as he looked up at me. I jumped off of Thunder and ran to Rufus, just as he collapsed into my arms. His stomach had erupted with blood. Black powder was all over his shirt. I put my hand to his stomach to stop the bleeding. It felt hot to the touch. Dealie held their new daughter, Laura, born just two weeks before. The baby was crying, and Dealie was screaming. "They took our cattle," she sobbed, "and they shot Rufus!"

"Who did?"

"Some men," she cried, "and then Rufus shot at them and they shot back. They were white men." Her feet were going up and down, jostling her baby. "Oh, my goodness, oh my goodness," she sobbed, "Is he going to live? Oh, my goodness, I was so scared."

"Get back inside, Dealie, and lock the door," I told her. "I know you're scared, but I've got to take Rufus into town to a doctor." I sat my brother on the steps.

"I'll go with you," she said.

"No. Please, get back inside, Dealie, and protect your baby." I tried to sound firm, but stuttered like I had an affliction. I could not think. I started talking in Choctaw, and then in Chickasaw. I am not sure she understood. "Himona," I asked her to wait. "Here, Dealie. Take his gun."

She took it, reluctantly and delicately.

"I am going to put Rufus on the back of Thunder and go to Mama to get the wagon. You get back inside and I will bring Mama, Lottie, and Mollie back to you. Get back inside, and render a prayer, fast. Do it now!" I shouted so she would know I meant it.

I wrapped Rufus's belly with the cloth I'd bought to make Laura's dress, tying it tight. He kept mumbling in Choctaw. I lifted him on Thunder, unsure whether doing that would not make the wound bleed more. I had to push hard to get him up there. He was taller and heavier, but I did it. I kept saying under my breath, "Lord, be with me," and, "Papa, please give me your courage and strength."

I got to Mama's place to find she and Lottie already had Blue hooked up to the wagon, where Mollie sat with a blanket. Mama said Rufus's horse was in the corral, but I could see it was Dealie's, not his. His was a paint.

Rufus mumbled that the thieves had stolen his horse. Mama helped me lay him in the wagon. I asked Lottie to keep pressure on the wound, and hauled Mama to Rufus's place to stay with Dealie and the baby. Lottie and I made it into Tishomingo after dark. I did not know where else to go but to the Brown's settlement, where I hoped to find Houston. Rufus was still bleeding, but not as much, and he was fading in and out of consciousness. I told Lottie to keep talking to him to help him stay awake.

"Talk to me," Lottie urged him. She had learned a few words in Choctaw and Chickasaw.

I heard him mumble in Choctaw to our God to save him, and keep him alive for his family. Tears built like rain on the sides of my cheeks. I had to stay brave.

At the Brown's home, Houston was outside moving stock. He got into the wagon, and guided us to the only person he knew could help us. She was not a doctor—the only doctor, who came from Ardmore, was not due for another week. She was a midwife, but Houston thought she could at least stop the bleeding.

Again, I faced loss and asked myself to be brave. And again, I looked at a moment when I did not know what tomorrow would be like. It was a night of prayer while the Chickasaw woman worked around the clock to save my brother.

Houston stayed and together we prayed. He said some new prayers in Chickasaw, and we held hands, waiting for news.

"Please let our brother be with us tomorrow. Please Aba Binili, help us stay together as a family," we prayed.

Close to morning, rain began to fall like a downpour of bloodshed. We continued our prayers, but Rufus did not make it to see the light of day.

THE MARRIAGE

It was a special day when Houston and I wed. He was most willing to please me and make me happy once again. I told him how important Lavina Frazier had been in my life and that I wanted her to be at my wedding. We paid a fee of two dollars to the Chickasaw Nation, and Albert McKinney from Emet recorded our marriage at the clerk's office in Tishomingo. Houston took me to the church at Blue Springs Prairie, near where the Fraziers lived. After we were married by the preacher Allen Wright, all three of us went to the home of the Fraziers, and partook supper.

"What kind of preacher are you?" I asked the Reverend Wright. "My papa was raised by missionaries, and he was a Methodist."

"I am a Presbyterian preacher for the Choctaws," he said.

"My Mama was Choctaw," I told him.

Houston put in, "Did you know, Esther, that the Reverend Wright translated many treaties into the Choctaw language, and was a Choctaw interpreter? And he got to go to Washington as a representative and translator."

I was impressed. "Oh my, Reverend. It was an honor to have you marry us."

Houston shared with me later that night that when the Choctaw-Chickasaw Treaty was set up under the name of the "territory of Oklahoma," the Reverend Wright was responsible for the name. He told the commission, as their translator, that the Choctaw and Chickasaw word, "okla," means people, and the word "homa" means red.

I also learned much about my husband that night. Everyone talked highly about Houston's career with the Mounted Regiment.

"Did you know, Esther," the Reverend Wright asked me, "that after the closing of Fort Washita near Milburn, the Mounted Regiment was dissolved?"

"I did not, Reverend," I replied again politely, feeling a little lost. All I had known was that Houston had been a part of it. The skills he learned must have helped him be a good constable for the Chickasaw Nation. I felt very proud.

He made very good money, which allowed us the blessing of help at the settlement. By our second year of marriage, I was with our first child. It felt good to be pregnant again.

Mama was busy helping Lottie with her new life, now that she'd found someone named Price. Dixon Frazier had passed away the year before, and I asked Lavina to move in with us. She came into our lives as our first daughter, Ella, was born. She was a lot stronger than Jessie, my child with Benjamin, had been, and so was I. Nursing her was easier, and I could tell I would have my hands full with her. Ella was active, spirited, and fun to care for. I found motherhood agreeing with me.

I would go into Tishomingo by wagon and pick up notions so Lavina and I could make clothing for Ella. Houston had traded for a new Studebaker wagon, with hub bands guaranteed never to come loose. He understood my anxieties after losing Benjamin. Besides, I assured myself that I looked quite good riding into town in my new wagon. I laughed at the thought of my papa pointing his finger at me for being so prideful. He always told me pride would get in my way.

Tishomingo was becoming quite a town. The Missouri, Kansas, and Texas Railroad ran between Boggy Depot and Tishomingo, bringing lots of strange-looking people there. The constables were supposed to enforce a tax on non-citizens, and even charge them a permit fee. Often you would see the men arguing with the constables about it. I was careful not to walk near them.

Houston told me the federal government's Act of 1871 was intended to get rid of tribal self-government. I told him my papa would not like me being here and knowing what was happening. I did not add that he had predicted some of it. Houston told me the law made Indians the "ward of the state, and removed all previous treaties." And it opened the opportunity for assault on Indian land titles. I became really worried about holding on to our lands.

I knew I would find Houston at his office working on such things when I came to Tishomingo, and although he never liked me to come alone, I had to tell him I was in town. And I wanted to know more about what was going on. My papa taught me to "be aware, Little Bird," and I was aware, especially that we could lose the land he had fought to keep for his whole life. Our first lands were taken away, and he came here to make this land our home. Now all the Indian Nations once again feared our lands would be taken. My heart ached.

In Houston's office on the second floor sat a tall white man with dark hair, talking to him. I walked around the corner and took a bench in the hallway. "Chukilissat binilili," I told myself to sit quietly.

I could see Pennington Creek running behind the buildings on Main Street. The rain that morning had been a hard one, leaving puddles, and wagons made ruts in the road. I walked to the window and saw a rainbow arching from behind the buildings to the west somewhere. It brought more memories of Papa, who told me the story of the "Great Rainbow" that "Chihowa," our God, created. It was in the shape of a bow, and it would always follow a big rain. It was God's bow and arrow, and a promise we would always have land. Papa said the arch, at the very top of the rainbow, was where our God would pull back his arrow. I loved that rainbow. I felt it was sending me a sign. It slowly disappeared behind the clouds and the buildings, and I saw the man walk out of Houston's office.

I recognized him as Preacher Raper from Milburn, and nodded to him. The sheriff, Mr. McKinney, who used to be the county clerk who recorded our marriage, also passed, tipping his hat.

Houston looked preoccupied. He touched my hand gently, and told me I should quickly get my business done in town, and go on back to the settlement. "Today is not a good day for you to be here." He was busy with laws and changes, and some men were there with not such good thoughts in their hearts.

He told me the Reverend Raper had come to tell him soldiers would come through Tishomingo in the next few days, and there might be some disruption among our people.

"Did that man know something of my brother's killers?"

"Maybe, Little Bird. We're not sure. We will probably never find them, but I will look into information he gave me about a white man he saw with what he thought was Rufus's horse—a paint pony." He squeezed my hand. "Sorry, Little Bird," he apologized. "I need to notify Sheriff McKinney and the other constables of the strangers coming into our Territory." He stood. "You need to go home." He walked me into the hallway.

I smiled and rushed out of the building, rendering a prayer to God to watch over all our people that day. I looked to "hushi," the sun gleaming through the clouds, and rendered a prayer my mama taught me. "Shilombish Holitopa Ma!"

My prayer to the Holy Spirit.

THE CATTLE BOOM

Houston was having a difficult time with cattle thieves. He wanted me to keep Ella close to the yard, and for me to carry my pistol at all times. I could remember the day I found Rufus shot by one, and Houston's vow to find his killer, and bring him to justice. I felt I somehow had put a great burden on this proud man that I married. "The cattle boom is changing everything around here," I told him.

"It has brought many intruders, sometimes dangerous men and thieves," he agreed, and observed, "With the annuity payments Governor Benjamin Overton got for the Chickasaws, many of our neighbors are hiring help with their land, instead of doing the work all by themselves."

"I don't want strangers coming to help us," I said.

"It's going to be all right," he assured me. "He said we were given enough to support us without relying on others."

"So, what happens to all our neighbors who don't have titles to their settlements?" I asked, frustrated. "These white men act like they have all the rights. The fencing they put up makes everyone angry."

"The white men come into our territory, steal our cattle, and then take it to their leased, fenced-off lands and claim the cattle to be theirs. It makes it harder for us constables to enforce the law," he frowned bitterly.

"*I know* that's what happened to Rufus's cattle and horse," I said.

"I am going to find that man one of these days, Esther," he said. He kissed me and headed out to work.

The day of chores began as usual. Thunder had developed a little arthritis in his front fetlock. I had rubbed poultice over his hooves the night before. Ella was at my heels that morning. She was used to being around the horses. She walked around me and Thunder as if we were all one. She was never still, just like I was never still, at her age.

"Settle down," I told her. "You are making Thunder restless." I moved her over to the side so I could work on his hoof. "Mama is trying to help his sore legs," I told her, a little more firmly. Be still. You have Chihowa Iowak, God's fire, just like I used to have."

She scurried past me, and I laughed and tried to grab. She pointed at me, and tried to say "Chihowa," but it came out nothing that anyone could understand except me. We often had a laugh when she told people she was Chickasaw. She would say, "I am Chick-a-Haw," shouting the "Haw," with a stomp.

I looked up and saw the three crows sitting at the far end of the stables. The larger one pecked and cawed, as if trying to get my attention. I wondered if these crows would ever get old, or if Aba Binili just sent a new batch every once in a while, to check on me. I did know I did not like the feeling that came over me when

I saw them, as if something was in the air that day in early June, while the warmth of Indian Territory was bearing down, bringing sweat to my forehead.

To my surprise I saw Houston riding down our path, several riders with him. I scooped Ella up and felt for the pistol in my apron pocket. I was not sure who the other men were. Houston slid off his horse and the others stayed back. I recognized his brother, Jerry.

"Chukma, Little Bird," Houston bent to kiss Ella's cheek, rushing past. "I have to get a few things from the house."

"What? What things?" I ran after him.

He told me that he, Jerry, Henry Bogle, and Johnson Keel were heading north. He said the Reverend Raper was right, that someone had seen Rufus's horse at a white man's ranch there. He packed some clothing and another pistol. He told me not to worry.

He told me, "Today I see the light. I see a path, Little Bird. I must take the path to find the man who killed Rufus. I saw your pain. Today I will try my best to honor you by finding justice. Today I must stand against the white man who took away your brother. We will capture this man, and bring your brother's horse home to his family."

I knelt at his feet, and begged him not to go. I feared another loss. He knelt to comfort me. "The crows were here today, it is a sign! It is *my* sign, a warning!" I cried and clung to him. "Please don't go, Houston!"

Ella scrambled to get between us.

"God will be with me," he told me. "I will come back home to you, I promise, Little Bird. I will come home to both of you." He kissed Ella on the forehead and walked out.

I rendered my prayer to God to travel with him and protect him. I waved to his brother and friends. They circled the yard and left.

Ella and I went to finish the chores. The day passed slowly, time moving like the waters of a frozen stream. Ella ran around the yard, with her hands out like wings. I smiled when she ran to me and called me "Little Bird," like Houston did.

"You are my Little Eagle, Ella," I called to her. She ran like a bird flies in the sky. I sat on the porch and watched the day slowly shift to dusk. I could see a rain squall coming from the southwest. The outlines of the three crows, following each into the top of a tree, caught my eye. They came to warn me of this day, I thought. I was glad Houston was headed north, away from the storms. I heard coyotes yowl to the east, and gathered Ella to feed her and lay down with her to try and rest. Lavina came across the pasture from Mama's settlement on her horse, and waved. Mama was not feeling well, and she had gone to attend to her.

The sun danced a circle around the clouds as daylight broke. A clear breeze dispelled the heat coming into daybreak, another morning in Indian Territory. A cottonwood tree close to the house whisked its branches against the house, making little crackling sounds, like a small fire burning. It was a fire. It was a fire in my heart, a pain of not knowing where my Houston was, or if he was safe. It was a pain my papa asked me to surpass. But again, I was having a day that challenged my bravery.

I had only slept but a few restless hours. I stood on the porch at sunrise, trying not to wake Ella, and saw sun dancers at a distance—horses moving in and out of the sunlight. I blinked, thinking I was seeing things. Their approach was powerful, and at their front was Houston. He towed a beautiful little paint pony—my Rufus's. I would know it anywhere. Jerry was with him, but I did not see Bogle or Keel. I stepped into the shadows of the cottonwood, reached my hands to the sky in praises, and kissed the wet, soft muzzle of my brother's horse.

Houston embraced me with the strength of a great warrior. He said, "We found your brother's killer. But he had already been slain by others. We left him there, but the men who killed him told us we could take Rufus's pony home."

"Who was he?" I asked,

"A cattle thief named Don Harrington," he said. "Harrington and his brother had stolen from others before." He reached a fist to the sky, "Justice has been done this day!" He bellowed.

"Who shot him?" I asked.

"A bounty hunter from Arkansas. He'll take him back for money," he said.

Jerry left for his settlement. Houston stayed home to rest and would file his report to the Chickasaw Nation in the morning. The night's rain had left a sweet smell of damp dew on the grass, and I looked out at his dew-softened footsteps in the grass, to cherish and relive again the sight of him coming home to me. Houston returned part of what was stolen from me, and from Rufus. My papa would be so proud this day. Tears filled my eyes and streamed down my face. I felt the release of my brother's pain and the pain of loss all at once.

Houston looked at me. "Let's remember this day." He continued, "To the white man, he sees nothing but the value of money that those cows brought to him. To the white man, he knows nothing of our pain. To me, I must as a Chickasaw man—I must be true to the soil from whence I came. Let's walk on our land with honor. Let's love one another with compassion. This Chickasaw Nation I am sworn to protect. This family I am sworn to protect. I will never leave you, Little Bird."

Two weeks passed before Houston came home with a subpoena from the Office of the United States Marshal, Western District of Arkansas, Fort Smith, to appear in court on August 10, 1877, for the murder of Don Harrington.

"What is going on, Houston?" I blurted to him. "Please, tell me."

"I will go to Governor Overton, and ask him what to do," he

said. Later that day he went to the office of the governor, and told me they would help him compose a letter with signatures of witnesses who knew he did not kill Mr. Harrington, saying that Mr. Harrington had already been killed by the bounty hunter, a man named William Brock.

I was grateful Houston took those men with him, and that there were witnesses.

We waited for over a month after the governor and Houston composed and sent the letter and the signatures in response to the subpoena. No one came to talk with Houston or the governor after that. Nothing ever came of it, and he wasn't subpoenaed again. But I knew he worried about it. He would lay beside me in bed and look at the ceiling in quiet contemplation. He was worried about accusing Brock of the murder in his letter. But the man had told Houston he killed Harrington, and willingly offered the pony back after he described it and told him how Rufus was killed. He wondered if the man was arrested because of his statement, or if Brock never received a bounty, or even may have lied about who he was. Maybe Brock had come to murder Harrington, and fooled Houston. I knew he weighed through all of these thoughts, because he was an honorable man.

I rendered a prayer that God would help him find peace.

THE QUESTIONING OF HENRY BOGLE (1902)

I was supposed to go to Muskogee, Indian Territory, to meet with the commissioners of the Five Civilized Tribes again in February of 1902, but it was a very far journey for me and eight-year-old Holmes. My daughters, Mattie and Francis, were in school at the Harley Institute, and Hattie had moved out after marrying a man named Orr. Ella was pregnant again and not able to travel. Belle was still recovering from the death of her husband. That left just me and little Holmes to go alone over a hundred and seventy-five miles by wagon. The trip would take five days with two horses pulling us. Instead, I went to Ardmore and got a lawyer named Thompson to represent me at the commissioners' meeting. Mr. Thompson said he would stop by to tell me what happened when he returned.

It was the middle of February, and my place had been neglected through the winter. My health was not good and I had my hands full with Holmes. I thought I heard a rider coming up the road. I went to the door to see our trees shadowing the front porch, big and bold with boughs bent low under the weight of the wintry wind. The sunlight sent a glow along the wooden floor reflecting up the logs stacked outside the door. I reached for my shotgun. Relieved, I recognized the rider as Mr. Thompson, I summoned Holmes to help tie up his horse.

"Chukma, Mister!" said Holmes, reaching for the reins.

"Hang on, son. Let Mr. Thompson get off his horse first," I warned Holmes. "Welcome, Mr. Thompson. I hope you had a pleasant ride."

"Yes, but today was a little colder than yesterday. I do hope that spring is not too far away." He tipped his hat.

"Come on inside out of the cold, and let me fix you some soup to heat up your innards." He gladly accepted my offer. I rolled up a log in my apron and carried it inside to stoke up the fire a little. I offered him a chair and Holmes took his coat. I gave Mr. Thompson his soup, and Holmes and I scooted our chairs close to the fire, to hear what he had to say.

"Well, Mr. Thompson, tell us about the meeting in Ardmore, please." Holmes dropped to the floor to sit cross-legged like he did when I was about to tell him one of my papa's stories.

"Mrs. McLish, we got there and they swore in a Mr. Henry Bogle as a witness on your behalf." He said the commissioners wanted to know when and where Bogle knew me. Mr. Bogle said he knew me in 1872 when we all lived near Boggy Depot. "Mr. Bogle explained that your husband Houston Brown was a full-blood Chickasaw Indian, and that he was enrolled as such."

"Did they ask Henry Bogle if I was married to Houston?" I inquired, knowing full well that they always asked if I was married to any of my husbands. It was a most common question. I knew that.

"Yes, they did. And they wanted to know if Bogle considered you to be Houston Brown's wife."

"I knew they would ask that. I also knew that they probably wanted to know if everyone in the neighborhood thought we were married." I wished I had gone to hear all this. But then again, it would have made me all upset in my emotional state. It was best that I'd stayed home.

"Are you sure you weren't hiding in a closet there?" The attorney smiled and winked.

"No, sir, I wasn't. But all their questions run about the same."

He handed me his bowl and asked for a bit more. I got him about a half a bowl and he ate a minute or two before he continued. "The commissioners wanted to know how long Bogle knew you and Houston. Bogle said he knew y'all over two years, and he went back to visit y'all in '76, when he stayed overnight. He told them he stayed about three days at your home, and that you had one child with you at the time. He said he did not know the child's name. They did repeatedly ask Bogle if y'all were married, and if that was y'all's child."

"That was my daughter, Ella, Mr. Thompson," I said. "You've met her."

"My sister," Holmes said, proudly participating like a grown-up.

"Yes, I know, son." Mr. Thompson smiled. "I was given the chance to question Mr. Bogle myself, so I asked him how old the child was, and if you were living in the Choctaw Nation at that time. Bogle explained that the child was about a year old, and that you were living in the Choctaw Nation. I also asked him if he knew if Houston Brown was full-blood Chickasaw and he answered, 'yes' once more. The only other thing I asked Bogle was if he was an intermarried Choctaw."

"He was intermarried Choctaw" I affirmed, "and he already

has his allotment."

"Yes, he confirmed that with me," the attorney added.

I thanked him for trying to help me out. He assured me that we would get through this and urged me to keep rendering my prayers.

Holmes went out to open the gate to the corral where we'd tied up his horse. The trees left a longer shadow across the yard, and the wind blew tumbleweeds around the fence. Mr. Thompson rode back up the road. Two crows cackled at the end of the fence post. One swooped around Mr. Thompson and back toward the house. I hurried Holmes out of the cold, and closed the door just as the other crow joined the two, to fuss their cold breaths into the wintry air.

"What are those fala saying, Mama?" Holmes asked.

"I think they're saying someone just gave out some truths about something," I replied.

"What truths, Mama?"

"I don't know, Holmes. But maybe Mr. Thompson can help us find some."

He wrapped his arms around my legs. "I sure hope so, Mama."

After the attorney Thompson left and I put Holmes to bed, I read Mr. Bogle's statement. I just sat down and cried again. I could not believe they had to ask such embarrassing questions of someone who was a friend, and who had stayed at our house. Bogle traveled with my Houston and he knew me. I am sure glad he was able to answer what they asked him, but I bet he was wondering why they questioned him so much. I rendered a prayer for Mr. Bogle and said a "thank you" for him and his family, that they had their allotment.

LOTTIE (1877)

I went to spend a day with Lottie and her husband.

"I am so happy to see you are feeling well," I said while she greeted me with a hug.

Lottie had married William Nathan Price in 1872, when Mollie was five. He was a very wealthy man who had moved from Mississippi and bought thousands of acres. He was an educated and wise cattleman, able to hire all the help Mama and Lottie would ever need. Mama was fifty-five and aging quickly.

Mama embraced me. "Well, Little Bird, I am so happy to see you. Ella, come see your Nana." She picked up her granddaughter.

"Mama, you put her down," I said, seeing her struggle to lift Ella. "She's a big girl, now."

Ella was my spirited child, and I was pregnant with my second one, so she would finally have a playmate. When I realized I was pregnant, I knew Aba Binili was paying me back for all the trouble

I caused Mama. "Now I have my little troublemaker, Ella, and she is definitely my Little Eagle," I told Momma and Lottie. Ella ran over to pull at my hand.

"Mama, tell me the story of the stomp dance," she begged.

"Ella, my child, there are so many stories. Why do you want to know the story of the stomp dance?"

She shuffled in a circle around me. "Please, Mama."

"All right, sit down at my feet, Little Eagle." She, Mama, Lottie and Mollie all sat down to hear me to tell the story. It was like old times, when Papa would tell us his stories.

"Once a long time ago the elders came together by the river, and they sat in a circle and prayed for the sick and shared stories of their families. Many of the elders knew that Aba Binili would want them somehow to render their prayers at the end of the circle meeting, and sing praises to our God for all His blessings.

"One day, while they sat in the circle, a beautiful butterfly came floating."

"Where did the butterfly come from?" Ella tugged at my skirt, wanting me to sit on the floor beside her.

"Be patient, my child, and I will tell you." I sat on the floor and continued my story.

"Aba Binili sent it. As the butterfly began to circle around one of the elders, who was singing praises to God for all our blessings, the elder stood and started to follow it. The butterfly wove circles around him, so the elder had to shuffle his feet to slow down and stay behind it.

"Another elder stood, and took the hand of the elder in front, and began to stomp and shuffle his feet while they both followed the beautiful butterfly. They repeated the song of praise as they stomped and shuffled. Soon, all the elders were holding hands and following the butterfly in the most beautiful circle of songs of praise and dance.

"From then on, at the end of the elders meeting, everyone would join all the elders in a big circle to begin their stomp dance, singing their praises to God.

"Sometimes, if we are lucky, the butterfly will make his most beautiful appearance. When the butterfly joins us, we all know it is a message from Aba Binili of his love for us," I said, concluding the story as I stood back up.

Ella jumped up and began to shuffle her feet while I sang the song of praise. I could feel the child within me move, like a soft drumbeat. I was so blessed that day, quiet in my thoughts of Papa, and how he taught me so much. It was good to share with my children.

Ella and I returned home late that afternoon, finished our chores and ate supper alone. Houston came in late that evening, and sat down with *The Vindicator*, the Choctaw paper, which he tried to read in Chickasaw. He gave up and handed it to me to read.

"Send our children to schools that can be carried on in a manner that would reflect honor on the Chickasaw Nation, besides doing a lasting good for the coming generations. Let us inaugurate schools that will elevate our children," I read to him.

He took my hand and said we needed to think about sending Ella to school someday. He said he remembered being at the meeting a few years back when Governor Overton signed an act establishing a female boarding school at Bloomfield Academy under the contract system. The contractors were Mr. Wharton, Mr. Boyd, and Mr. Johnston. Houston was friends with Mr. Johnston, and said the school was looking for children of good moral upbringing. "I think when Ella is six, we can think about sending her."

I was not sure about a boarding school. I thought the whole idea would separate Indian families and was another way white men could remove us from our families. Our culture could be lost. I told him the whole idea concerned me, and besides, we had Lottie's husband to help teach our children.

He laid his hand on my stomach. "The boy is kicking you," he said and laughed.

"So, Houston, how do you know we are having a boy?" I brought his hand up and kissed it.

"We need an intrepid warrior in the house." He smiled.

"We already have one warrior in the family. I think Ella needs another girl to play with." I smirked a little.

"I am not sure we can handle three birds in this house." He raised his arms, like a bird in flight. "We have Little Bird, and Little Eagle. But I am ready for a 'Little Hawk' to be my son."

"Well, don't hold your breath. This baby moves around just like Ella did. I hope you will not be disappointed with a girl," I said as I stood to get his supper.

"Whatever we have, it will be God's blessing, and I will love it—intrepid warrior, or brave hawk."

"Oh, you will? A warrior or a hawk, huh? But I have already named our new daughter."

"And what would that be?" He raised an eyebrow.

"She will be named Belle," I said, like I knew for sure. "My papa told me the story about this beautiful bell that Chief John Ross of the Cherokees brought to Fort Gibson and put in the mission church at Park Hill. Papa thought greatly of John Ross, he was Papa's minko. You remember, my papa was a minister?" I brought Ella to the table. "Papa told me that when he saw them carry that bell into the church and heard its amazing sound, he knew our ancestors were glorifying God. My next daughter will be my Belle."

"Well, we will see, Little Bird," he chuckled. "I do like the sound of the name 'Belle.'"

I told him of our day with Lottie and Mama.

"How was it hanging around in the white man's world?" His question dripped with prejudice.

"Now, Houston, Lottie loves Nathan a lot, and he is very good to her," I replied, touching his hand.

"Well, I am glad she is happy," he said, trying to sound nice. "I know she was a very sad woman when Tuskatubby was killed, but she has a daughter to raise. At least Price isn't like most of those white cattle ranchers who come in just to steal our lands."

"Even though he was a big cattleman, he moved here to teach," I said. I laid my head on his shoulder.

"Well, you know, the talk around the settlements is," he said, with a pause, "that these white men have come to seek marriage of convenience with Chickasaw women. I sure hope this Price man is not one of them."

"Oh, Houston, I think most of these men who come to work in the schools are trying to obey the laws of our people," I said. "Remember, my papa came with other white missionaries to help our Indian brothers and sisters." I went to clean off the table.

He continued, "And some were accused of abusing the privileges of their wives because they wanted the rich grassland these Indian women owned, to feed the cattle that they brought with them."

"Oh, that's enough talk about these white men," I said.

But he went on, "And a lot of whites are using the Chickasaw easy adoption policy to lay claim to shares in the Chickasaw Nation's funds."

"Oh, Houston. I am so proud of you. You are such a good man and a smart man," I told him. "But it is time for you to stop thinking of all this matter and get some rest."

I took the lantern and his hand, and led him off to bed.

THE HANGING

In 1878, midwives were commonly used and Houston preferred that I use one for the delivery of my second daughter, Belle. But whether to use one or not was an argument we did not get to have. My water broke early, and Lavina helped me through delivery. It took a little longer for Belle to come into this world, but she rang out her "bell" of a cry the moment she entered Indian Territory. I knew Papa would be proud of her name. She sang a beautiful sound, like none other I have heard.

Lavina had met a Mr. King in Tishomingo and fell in love. After Belle was a couple of months old, she moved out. It was good for her to start her life again. Dixon was a wonderful man, but she had lost him at a young age, and I was proud she was able to begin her life again. However, I was a little frustrated because I was raising two little ones with no help.

The settlement was now full of workers and fewer chores were imposed on me. I had become my Mama, with the cooking and the children, and very little time for my love of horses. Thunder would nicker to me from the field, and I would long to ride him again.

Mama was still not in the best of health, and wanted to go back to Tennessee to see her family. We feared for her to travel, but once enough men were hired to help with both properties, she left for Chattanooga. I prayed for her a safe journey, as she found another family that wanted to travel to Tennessee with her. I gave them my best wagon and Houston ordered another. Mr. Owens out of Atoka made a new harness for it.

There had been a trial the previous December, wherein a man named John Wheat was convicted of killing a Creek man named Torrey. Torrey had fired at Mr. Wheat several times before Mr. Wheat killed Torrey. But the jury did not believe his plea of self-defense, and found him guilty of murder. He was sentenced to hang at the Chickasaw Nation's jail in Tishomingo. On the morning of the execution, Houston told the girls and I that we were not allowed to come to town. Later, when the girls were asleep, he told me the details of Mr. Wheat's execution. Wheat had walked out onto a scaffold, his wrists and his ankles bound. He told the witnesses he would see them all again in heaven and still protested that he shot the man in self-defense. He said he tried to serve the Lord, and asked for forgiveness of his sins. A deputy pulled a black hood over his head, and adjusted the noose around his neck. The trap door opened, and he fell to his death.

"Dr. Trout monitored his vital signs and pronounced Mr. Wheat dead," Houston finished.

"Oh, Houston, that was a terrible thing to witness," I gasped at the thought of it and reached for his hand. "I know why you asked me to stay home."

He shuddered. "It was just awful," he said and sank down into the chair next to me.

I rendered a prayer with him that this poor man would rest in peace. I now understood what Houston meant when he spoke about capital punishment. I hoped our girls would never have to see such a horrific scene.

Still, I looked forward to going into town and seeing new faces. Not everyone was excited about more white people coming to Indian Territory. But the Irish seemed really nice, with their awkward talk and their bright red hair. I laughed at some of the men who came into town, wearing the plaid skirts of their homeland, although I knew I should not. I am sure they saw us as strange, too. The Irishmen soon learned to dress more like the English, and were all good cattle ranchers. They seemed to really want to make a go of the land, some bringing their own herds of cattle or money to buy them. Houston respected the ones who tried hard to obey our Indian laws.

I watched the sun rise one morning from my front porch. Ella decided to entertain Belle with stomp dances and songs, so she paraded around the baby lying on a blanket in the sun. Houston had left early for a meeting with the sheriff about a man suspected of larceny. Afterwards, he and the other constables were to discuss "capital punishment," which to me just meant "death." I had not forgotten the story of Mr. Wheat, and rendered a prayer to our God to watch over our people and to keep Houston brave.

The day passed quickly while I made a new dress for Ella. She was to go into town with me soon to interview with the new schoolmaster, to see if she was ready to go to school. I had asked Nathan to help with some things she needed to know. I was still upset about the idea of her having to live at a school. It was something I do not think my papa would have approved of, but I wanted her to be well educated.

The evening sun passed down a golden red. There was nothing like the beauty of a sunset in Indian Territory. I watched up the path, and the land swelled into a mound of darkness. I longed to see Houston riding in from work. Nightfall came with no word and no sound of him. I dozed in a chair by the fire until I was startled by a knock at the door. I jumped and reached for the pistol in my apron pocket.

"Who goes there?" I cracked the door, pistol pointed at the figure on the porch.

"Mrs. Brown," the Indian man said. "My name is Jim Wolf." He sounded hesitant.

"Chukma," I said. "My husband is not here right now and I would prefer that you come back another day when he is, Mr. Wolf."

"Mrs. Brown, I am the jailer for the Chickasaw Nation. My name is Jim Wolf," he said again. I detected reluctance in his tone.

"I recognize your name, Mr. Wolf. I believe we have met before. I have heard Houston speak of you—but again, he is not here right now." I very much wanted him off my porch and on his way. I did not want the girls awakened.

"Mrs. Brown, I am here to tell you that your husband has been shot by a man who is now a criminal at large." He sighed. "I am so saddened to bring you this news of betrayal and violation of character, but Mr. Brown is no longer with us."

I must have collapsed into his arms. I saw him standing over me. He held me up.

"Oh, no," I screamed. "My Houston is not gone. He can't be. You must be mistaken. He was just here this morning. We have two little girls. He would never leave me. Please, please tell me Mr. Wolf, this cannot be true." I clung to his shirt like a bear.

Ella came from her bed to my side, crying because of my screams. Mr. Wolf took us in his arms and held us while we cried our hearts out in pain. Ella did not know why she was crying. She was only five, but her mama was crying. She could feel my pain.

"God, please, please," I screamed. "Why is this happening to me again?"

I felt the deepest part of pain. Why was Aba Binili punishing me? I was a good woman, good to my family and my husband. I was older, and I knew this Chickasaw man I loved was brave, and would never leave me and my children. He was my strength, like my papa. I prayed far into the night for someone to come wake me from the nightmare, and must have fallen asleep, at last.

In my dream, I saw an Indian man with a painted face, looking into mine. He was shaved, and looked ready for war. He held a spear, pointed at my skull. His foot pushed heavily on my chest, which felt like it might explode. I screamed in fear.

I bolted up, my blanket wrapped like skin around me, Ella screaming beside me. My chest was hard and tight, but not from the Indian man's foot. I realized it was my breasts, full of milk. I had slept past time for Belle's nursing. Ella clung to me, sobbing. I went to the door, and saw Mr. Wolf stoking the fire. He asked me if I was all right.

It was real. My life was real. I was twenty-three years old, and I had lost two husbands, my first child, my papa and my brother. I cursed the sweet land Papa and Mama brought me to live on. I cursed the men who came to steal it all from us. I did all of it under my breath, hoping this man I barely knew would not hear me.

I rendered a prayer to God to help me forgive and be brave again. I asked him to forgive me for whatever sin caused me such terrible pain and loss.

I felt awkward to have this man in my house. Then I looked into both of my beautiful daughters' faces, one clinging to my leg and another to my chest. I excused myself from Mr. Wolf to a room of privacy to feed and care for them. I heard him step onto the porch. The man who just brought sorrow to me, the man who knew my Houston well, the man who journeyed to give me my bad news, was leaving me all alone. I felt panic, not wanting him to leave me. But he stayed.

"Be brave, Little Bird," I felt my papa say. I clung to my babies, and rendered prayers against the pain that overcame me. I prayed for my Houston, not knowing why he died, or what happened to him. I prayed until I must have fallen into the deepest slumber, with my babies clinging to me, their only hope for survival.

TWILIGHT OF THE STORM

I awoke and eased off the bed, trying not to disturb my two girls. I could hear the rain soft against the porch. I saw flashes of lightning. Thunder rumbled in the distance, the skies moaning my pain. The flickering light offered a faint semblance of hope, as if trying to settle me with jolts of truth. I knew I could not lay here all day. I had to put Houston to rest. The man named Wolf waited in the next room for me to make some sign of life.

He coughed loudly, to let me know he was there. He cracked the door and looked in on me and the girls.

"Excuse me, Mrs. Brown," he said softly, as he glanced past me at the babies sleeping. He asked if we would like something to eat.

"Yakoke," I responded in thanks.

Ella jumped up and ran toward the light in the doorway. Another boom of thunder and she bolted back into my arms.

The thunder made me clamp my teeth and I gritted them in

pain. I tried to smile, and not reveal my suffering. Another burst of thunder and I jumped. I closed the door, whispering, "Give us a moment."

We changed and washed our faces in a basin by the bed. I knew I must recover quickly, for the sake of my children.

A tiny bit of light flickered under the door. It grew dimmer and I hoped the darkness would engulf my pain. Our shadows flickered and I saw them like ghost dancers moving around a fire. That was how I conjured images of the past to ease the pain of present loss. I recalled the dream of that evil warrior and shook my head to remove the thought. And then I recalled another dream I had of Benjamin coming to comfort me, our little girl Jessie beside him, telling me my life would be okay, that I must be a brave "little bird," and hold onto life for the sake of my babies, to bring them into the light. His soft touch sent shivers down my arm, as I remembered. I looked at the back of his neck and his long hair flowing as he walked away from me. I could smell him in the room and knew he must have been there through the pain, to comfort me.

In the silence and stillness I gasped, grabbed Ella's hand, and carried Belle through the door, to light and food and life. There was no turning back. I laid down my suffering. It was a time to be brave, once again.

Mr. Wolf offered a chair. "Binili," he politely asked to sit.

He'd cooked up some rabbit stew, and it was quite tasty. It was good to have him there, even if I still felt uncomfortable. I did know of him, but I did not know this Chickasaw man.

He apologized and before I could respond, he offered, "I will go and get your sister and family and have them come here to be with you. I was in fear last night of leaving you here with your babies alone."

All I could do was nod.

He assured me he would bring Houston home for a proper burial.

"Where do you reckon they will want to bury him?" I asked.

He didn't really answer. "Because Mr. Brown was a constable, the governor will want to come to pay his respects," he said, "and to you and your children at the time of his burial." I think he was tired and nervous about having been with us for so long.

"Yakoke, Mr. Wolf," I thanked him. "Please go to my sister and family and bring them here to me, once the storm has passed. My mother is on a trip to Tennessee. Would you please send a message to Lavina King? She lives in Tishomingo."

Mr. Wolf walked to the corner of the room, where laid a leather pouch and a rifle. He carried them to me. "This is Mr. Brown's rifle and some of his things," he said.

I tried hard to not look on them. "Oh, yes. That's Houston rifle and a leather pouch he made when he first became constable," I said. "Yakoke."

I quickly turned away, so as not to see him holding the gun my Houston held just the day before. It was most upsetting that I had to think of my Houston's things as just things, now. I realized at that very moment that I would never be able to see his handsome face again. I turned back to the table, pretending to eat.

Jim Wolf told me how my constable, Houston Brown, was shot. He spoke softly, so as not to disturb the girls. He said Houston rode with a deputy to the home of a man named Dyer, the one who was accused of larceny. "You know, Mrs. Brown, one of his duties would be to arrest this full-blood Chickasaw man, Safron Dyer, for his crime," he said, almost pridefully.

I nodded that I understood.

"As he and his deputy got to Dyer's house, they held their Winchester rifles ready." He gestured like he held a rifle himself. "The deputy told me they saw the front door was open a crack, and as soon as Mr. Brown stepped onto the porch, Dyer shot him in the chest." He saw my face turn red and flush. He reached out to touch my hand. I moved it away. He lowered his head in apology. "So sorry, Mrs. Brown," he said. "Are you all right?" He leaned away.

"Yes, Mr. Wolf," I said. "Please tell me what happened."

"I reckon he died instantly," he sighed. "I am so sorry, Mrs. Brown." He rushed to finish the story. "The deputy was shot twice."

"Is he going to be okay?" I asked, with deep concern in my heart. "I will render prayers for the deputy and his family."

"Yes, he was able to get back to Tishomingo on his horse and tell the sheriff," Wolf continued. "But first he dropped back, even though the man Dyer was still shooting at him. He wanted to go back to get Mr. Brown, but he was not able to. The sheriff and some other deputies went back to Dyer's place, and recovered Mr. Brown and his horse. I put his horse in the corral when I got here," he continued.

"Yakoke," I thanked him again, trying to hold back tears.

"There is a manhunt now for Dyer. That is why I did not want you to stay here by yourself." He put Houston's rifle back in the corner. "Do you know how to use this?" he asked.

"I can use that rifle as good as any man," I assured him. "I will be all right. Thank you." I looked at the rifle and felt emptiness. It meant nothing to me. It would never bring my Houston back. I heard the rain. He could see I was starting to feel upset again. I really did not want him to leave until I could stop my trembling. But I knew I needed to be alone.

He excused himself to get his horse and move on to let the rest of my family know, and bring them to me.

I felt terrible that he left in the rain, but a little glad after the door closed behind him. My lower lip trembled. My skin crawled, and my heart pounded against the thought of what was happening to me. I closed my eyes and imagined Houston's face, which always seemed to calm me. I started to cry, doubting what my papa told me about my life, the next life, a better life. I now could pronounce Houston dead. I mourned, wailing like a warrior with an arrow deep in my flesh. Ella cried and held my legs. Belle wailed with me, as if her 'bell' was reaching out to her father in heaven. The darkness embraced us and held us there in our pain and sadness.

I could hear the rain fading into the wind, which somehow caused my crying to stop. I opened the door and breathed the dampness and cool of an October breeze. I looked out at our land, our home, our settlement. I took in very slow, deep breaths, watching droplets of autumn rain trickle from my roof onto the porch.

I knew death was not the end of someone. It was the beginning. Another life would follow, as Papa told me. Papa never lied. He would tell me the birds, and the horses, and the flowers die, but they go back into the soil and a newness of life always followed death. He told me that and I believed him. I knew about death. He shared his stories of the Trail of Tears that killed much of his Cherokee family while they moved into Indian Territory. He taught me to be sensible about death, but now I was living in death. So much death and gloom. I prayed that Papa would help me keep my faith strong.

I saw my three crows on the corral fence. One looked at me, iridescent feathers glistening like he was sweating tears. He bobbed his head and cawed like a scolding parent.

"Leave me, fala," I said. "Stop reminding me of my pain." I turned away and started to close the door. "Get," I shouted.

I waved and two crows flew off. The third paced along the corral fence.

I closed the door to the sound of the fading caws of the "truth talker," bellowing of death.

PEOPLE, ROADS, GUNS, AND RULES

Mr. Wolf made sure Houston had a most honorable burial. He introduced me to Governor Overton. He helped my family and seemed a man of integrity, although much quieter than any I had known. It was hard to understand what he might be thinking.

"How are you doing, Mrs. Brown?" he asked while he helped me and the girls into the wagon after the burial.

"I am doin' a bit weakly, but comfortable in my sorrow," I said. I was not sure he knew what I tried to say.

"Please send for me, if you need anything at all," he said. "Mr. Brown was a very fine constable and we all miss him." He lowered his head and backed away. I realized he was a much smaller man than I remembered and looked kind of frail.

Jim Wolf spent a lot of time on the road as the Chickasaw Nation's jailer, but when he was in town he would often come to the settlement to help me. I kept most of our help that Houston had hired to run the cattle and Jim seemed to know how to manage that part of our life. He gradually fit into our lives and the girls were comfortable with him. We called each other Mr. Wolf and Mrs. Brown for almost a year.

"May I call you Esther?" he asked one evening, after telling my girls good night before he headed back to Tishomingo.

"I think it is time for you to call me Esther," I said. "But what shall I call you, Mr. Wolf?"

"Why, Jim is my name. I would be most happy to have you call me Jim." He smiled a smile like I had not seen since Houston's death a year before.

The following summer of 1880, Jim Wolf and I decided to marry. He was a good friend to me and a great father to my girls. I wasn't sure at the time that I was in love with him. But I did come to love the man. He was there for me and my two small children when we needed it most, and respected their father.

Palmer Mosley, who would much later become governor of the Chickasaw Nation, married us at the capitol building in a quiet ceremony, with just my two girls there, along with Lottie and her husband.

I wore a special dress Lavina had made for me years ago, one I had kept in a box under my bed. It was full of colorful ribbons. I was twenty-five and had decided it was time to find my way into a life renewed. Jim Wolf was a good man and a fine, well-respected Chickasaw citizen. I had to continue my journey in life and to do as my papa had taught me. I was going to be brave and strong and find love in my life again.

I asked him one day, while we were reading the Bible to the girls, "What do you like about me, Jim?"

"Well, Esther, I like you because you are a strong woman." He continued, "And a woman with big dreams."

"So, you saw me at my weakest, and you still think I am strong?"

I asked.

"Your dreams for the future of our people are big, Esther. I wanted to share those dreams with you," he said.

He told me he wanted great things for my children and the children we may have together. He would walk beside me in a way no other man did before, with strength, although he made me believe he thought himself much stronger because I was at his side. That gave me a good feeling. I believed I was finally becoming what my papa expected me to become—a brave woman, with honesty and integrity.

In early fall, the girls and I went to Tishomingo to get supplies, leaving town late so we could go see Jim at work. We met him at the capitol steps.

"What a surprise," he said.

"We wanted to come see you at work. We just needed to get some things and tell you what I have been thinking," I said and smiled. I felt a renewed love in my heart.

"What are you thinking, Esther?" He took my hand and we walked down the steps of the capitol.

"Well, Mr. Jim Wolf, I think today is a beginning of a great life. We will build on a new family in this beautiful town of Tishomingo," I said. "I feel this is the best happiness anyone could ever have."

"Oh, you feel that, eh, Esther?" Jim chuckled and took Ella up in his arms.

"Come on, girls. Let's go home, and Papa Jim will kill a rabbit so Mama can make us some rabbit stew."

"Oh, Mama, please don't kill the little rabbit." Ella reached for me to take her from the bad man who was supposed to kill a rabbit.

"It's okay, Ella. Mama will make us pashofa instead, and leave the rabbit to roam the fields and eat up my garden." I turned to Jim with a wink.

We laughed. Laughter was such a good feeling and the girls

were seeing me smile a lot more. We crossed the swinging bridge at Pennington Creek and stopped for a look at the Blue Hole. Wagons rolled along the street, many people coming and going. It was a busy place, this Tishomingo. I could see at a distance the cabin of Jackson Frazier, Benjamin's cousin, built near Mill Pond at Pennington Creek.

Mr. Harlan, the postmaster, walked by and tipped his hat.

"Chukma," Jim said to Mr. Harlan.

"Good afternoon," Mr. Harlan replied.

"Oh, I almost forgot. I need to stop by the post office and see if my mother sent me a letter," I said.

We got into the Studebaker wagon Houston had ordered just before he was killed and Jim drove us over to the post office and I went in to check on the letter, but there was none. I felt like a new family was formed that day. It was a day I had painted in my mind years ago, seated on a rock by a stream when land was free and everyone walked in peace with each other. I saw my children's faces in that stream of water and now I saw them beside me. I knew I must travel into this new, changing world with my children, and teach them to hold on the ways of our people. I wanted to ensure this land remained ours and would never be taken away. I would try to be brave while our land changed, from open ranges to yards filled with people, roads, rules, and guns.

Indian Territory presented a greater challenge for my people. The white man's laws overrode many of ours. We came here as a farming people, and now had to understand growth, and see our prosperity not as a matter of who we were, but what we had. I wanted only the best for my children and Jim Wolf.

We passed Lottie's place on the way home. A neighbor girl, Lilla Turnbull, waved us down.

"Please come quickly, Missus Esther. Your sister Lottie is very sick, and needs you," She sounded frantic.

We drove on down to my sister's settlement. Nathan came out to the porch, wiping his brow. Their eight-year-old son Nelson came out, running and crying. I knew Lottie was pregnant, but her baby should not have been born for another month.

Mollie came out, carrying a baby wrapped in a blanket.

"Oh, the baby is here," I called out, joyfully. But everyone looked at me and shook their heads.

Nathan sobbed. He said Lottie gave birth too early, and he could not leave to find a midwife, nor could anyone find me. He and Mollie had done the best they could. "Oh, Esther, we lost Lottie and our baby boy."

I fell to my knees. I could not stop the pain. I felt I was going to be sick. "No. No. This can't be true! Why, oh, my Lord, do you continue to take my family from me?"

It had been such a happy day starting over with Jim, and now another loss. The girls piled on me, crying. Nelson wrapped his arms around me. I knelt on the dirt and reached a hand to the earth, the soil from whence I came, and ran my fingers through it, leaving marks of anger and frustration.

Jim pulled me up. "Stand up, Esther," he said. He reached for my hands. They were balled into fists. He spread them and hugged me, hard. "We have matters to take care of for your brother-in-law, here, and your sister and their child," he whispered in my ear, with great warmth and the sternness of a courageous man. "Be brave, Esther. Your family needs you right now." He picked up Belle and Ella.

Nathan took his baby son from Mollie and she turned to walk with us onto the porch and into my sister's home of sorrow, to give her our final love and respect.

No crows followed us home that day in Indian Territory.

WOLF AND FAMILY

One Friday afternoon, I sat on the porch in my rocking chair, feeling a special loneliness at not having my sister or my brother with me. On my lap lay a letter from my aunt in Tennessee, explaining that my mother had fallen ill and passed away the year before. I had read this letter three times, wiping the tears from my eyes. I was feeling sorry for myself over so many losses. I hated not knowing, until it was too late, that my mother had passed, not being there to bid her farewell. I listened to my husband's reassurance, I must be strong for the living. I believed I could be a good wife for Jim Wolf, if I could just keep myself away from such sadness. I tried hard to remember the family I had lost. I knew it was time to fill my days with the newness of life.

I often tried to turn my interest to Jim's work for the Chickasaw Nation. It was one way my papa taught me to move on with the times. Jim brought home a copy of the law that set out what his duties and responsibilities were. I had asked him for a copy on the day we married.

"I cannot believe you remembered to bring this to me, Jim Wolf." I smiled at him and gave him a kiss on the cheek.

Jim was always amazed at my interest in his career. I thought it was important that I understood what his job was. I was his wife and the one who honored him in all his work. I wanted to learn more about the man I married. "Esther, you always ask very little of me," he said. "It is my pleasure."

"Here, come sit beside me at the table and I will read this out loud," I said.

He was always amazed at my ability to read. I told him my father was a minister, educated by white men, and often would read the Bible to me, my brother, and my sister. That made me determined to learn to read like him. Papa also always wanted to know what was happening with the new laws in Indian Territory. Jim came to know I was definitely my father's daughter.

I read "*An Act Providing for a Jailer*," through the part that said, "*the Jailer shall receive into custody, and safely keep, subject to the order of the proper court, all offenders against the Laws of this Nation, who may be committed to his charge by any lawful officer, and the Jailer perform the duties incumbent on the Sheriff or Constable of Tishomingo County, Chickasaw Nation.*" I paused there.

"What's wrong?" he asked.

"So, this is why you and Houston became such good friends?" I asked. "Was the closeness because of your work?"

"Yes, Little Bird. We worked closely, but not at the capitol offices a lot. It was mostly on the road. He spoke often of his family, of you, and I know he loved you very much." He smiled and stretched. "Achakali," he asked me to continue.

I began again, through a part that read, "*the Jailer shall reside* in sight of the Jail; he shall see to the feeding of all prisoners in his charge; he shall supply them with good water three times per day. He shall perform all the duties necessary for the health and comfort of the prisoners." I paused again. "So, you are supposed to live at the jail and make those criminals comfortable?" I felt a little confused, because Jim always came home on nights he worked in Tishomingo.

"We have guards that stay at the jail at night now, Little Bird," he explained. "I will always be here for you, not to worry," he added.

I continued, "the Jailer shall receive the sum of three hundred dollars per annum, for his services as Jailer, and shall receive the sum of fifty cents per day for each prisoner's board while in his charge."

"Oh, I am so proud of the money you make, Jim Wolf." I reached for his hand. "We are surely blessed." I rendered a silent prayer of thanks.

We chuckled over section nine, which put the capitol's furniture under his protection, although we both knew it was important.

"Thank you, Jim, for bringing this home."

He put the paper back in the leather case he carried to work. "We will raise our girls to be good Chickasaw citizens." He took my hand, an assurance of his loyalty to me and the girls.

I was quite pleased with his job and his salary. It was a good job for him to have, and I felt enlightened to know more about the responsibilities that my husband had been given by the legislature as National Jailer.

Jim would often leave early in the morning for Tishomingo, which he still called "Good Spring." Sometimes I would hook my horses to the Studebaker and wander into town, where so many new people arrived by train or stagecoaches. My girls and I would watch these new people roll into town from the side of the hill.

The stagecoach was pulled by four horses, and we were told that it could go very fast. We agreed it was probably too fast for us.

Mr. G.W. Allen managed the mercantile store. I used to bring him rope made by Houston's father, named "Panachi," Chickasaw for cordage or rope maker. He and Houston had left a barn full of ropes.

I made rope, too. I would pull tail hair from our horses to twist into the cord and the cotton. It would take me a week or more to make thirty or forty feet of rope to sell to Mr. Allen. I also taught Ella, who liked that her papa used to do the same with his papa.

"Mama, tell me the story of Papa and the rope." She puffed up her cheeks every time she demanded that of me. In fact, she proclaimed everything strongly, an exhibit of some of her mother's worst traits.

So, on the ride into town, I retold the story to Ella and Belle. Ella referred to Panachi as Grandpapa, so I used that for his name.

"Grandpapa's hands were big, even though he was a little man. He would make the rope flow through the room when he twisted and twirled the cord," I told her.

And so, the story goes:

There once was a brave warrior. Many young warriors followed him into battle. The warrior always carried a long, brown cord made of horse hair, wrapped around his waist. He would never leave for battle without it.

One day his son asked him, "Papa, why do you carry so long a cord on your waist to go into battle?"

His father said, "I am a cordage maker. I am the 'brave of the brave.' I carry my cord because it will save my life and others' lives.'"

"'How do you know this, Papa?' the son asked him.

"Because, my son, the cord is my arrow, the cord is my sword, the cord is my Great Father's blessing to save me from any danger.'"

"How is that, Papa? It is just a cord! It is not magic. What can a cord do?"

"When I must catch an evil man, running away from me, I throw my cord, and trip him. When I catch this evil man, my cord will tie him up, or it will hang him from a tree for his crime. If I must shoot a deer for meat, my cord will tie the deer to my horse, so I can take the meat home to our family. And if I must get away from a bear or a mountain lion, my cord will hoist me up a tree or a rock to safety. My cord is most important for me to be a very brave warrior."

And so, his son understood the importance of the cord.

Ella smiled and turned quiet and intense while we rolled into town to trade cord for material to make dresses. We had money, but not as much as when I was married to Houston.

Inside the store, I noticed a man arguing with Mr. Allen about something. The girls and I skirted on past them, and I laid the cord on the front counter. I went to look at cloth for the girls' dresses.

I could tell Mr. Allen was getting upset. They were arguing about cattle. Then the man shook his fist at Mr. Allen, and I decided it was time for us to leave. I looked around for the girls. Belle, with her long black hair flying, hung onto my skirt tail, but Ella was nowhere to be seen.

"Ella, where are you?" I called out, not too loudly, hoping not to be noticed. I dragged Belle one way and another, and at last went back to the counter to grab the cord. It was gone.

And then I saw my daughter Ella, at eight years old, had taken it and quietly wound it around the angry man's leg, wrapping it in a most uncomfortable manner. I thought he would topple into Mr. Allen's arms.

"Oh, Ella," I shouted. "What are you doing?"

The man, unsure what to do, looked down at Ella. Then he began to laugh, although I could not tell whether he did so out of surprise or anger.

Mr. Allen laughed, too.

"That is a fine cord you have there, little girl," the man said, still laughing.

Mr. Allen unwound the once angry man, now a laughing man.

Ella came running to the other side of my skirt tail.

"Oh, Mr. Allen, I must apologize for my daughter's improper behavior and actions." I pulled Ella close. "Why did you do that, my child?" I reproved her.

"Mama, I'm a brave warrior and cordage maker, just like Grandpapa." She stepped away and raised her head and arms to the heavens.

Both men laughed again, but I was flustered at her prideful behavior. "You apologize, right now, Ella Brown Wolf, to these gentlemen." I said. I realized at that moment I was not to be surprised by anything this child would do, ever again. She had the makings of her mother, so she came by those most unpredictable characteristics honestly. I rendered a most quiet and internal prayer that we could get away as quickly and quietly as possible.

That did not happen.

The man bought the cord from Mr. Allen at double the price. Mr. Allen gathered up all the material I was looking over and gave me twice what I needed for the girls' dresses, in a most insistent manner. He thanked Ella and me, again and again. I guess the angry man decided to pay the price Mr. Allen was asking for the cattle, and for some odd reason he believed Ella was the cause for that miraculous change.

It was definitely time for the Studebaker, our horse, and the girls and I, to make our way home.

THE STORIES

It was Jim's job to lock up the capitol building and he often ran late getting home for supper. He never knew when the courts might adjourn, so we kept suppers warm for him. He was rarely home before the girls were ready for bed, but I tried to keep them up as long as I could so they could have time to visit. He was proud of them and would try to answer their questions about his day at work. Of course, I didn't wish him to scare them with tales of robbers and bandits. The girls saw matters differently, though.

"Mama, when will Papa Jim be home to tell us more stories about the bad men?" Belle would ask.

"Oh, Belle, you always want to hear Papa Jim's stories. But sometimes they make me have bad dreams," Ella scolded her.

"Now girls, don't bother Papa Jim so much about stories." I knew he would be so tired when he got home.

Jim tried to tell stories about light and simple crimes, if any.

But I knew he spent days with those convicted of much worse. Some would escape and Governor Overton would offer a reward, sometimes up to five hundred dollars, to bring them back to the Chickasaw Nation's jailer. Jim said many wanted help because of the bounty, although they were often of shady character themselves.

Ella and Belle loved to hear him tell the story of an old witch who lived in Devil's Den when he was young. Devil's Den was five miles north of Tishomingo, full of gigantic boulders. You could not find the Devil's Den by wagon. Bounty hunters would often head there to chase down and capture escaped criminals.

As Jim told the story, the old witch was evil. She would make the wolves howl and the owls fly low when she came out of the rocks. The people blamed her for a plague of bad health that had fallen on many of the babies after the Removal. He said a young man saw her one day and told the old minko, Emoklotubby, that he needed to kill her to stop the plague.

So, the minko went to the place, and climbed high on the rocks to wait until he saw the witch. He had brought his polished horn bow, and had dipped the tip of his arrow in poison.

A boisterous owl flew down in front of him and he turned so quickly he fell between two rocks. The arrow released from the bow before he could point it. It flew high in the air, barely missing the owl, and falling far behind it. He pulled himself up on the boulder again to see the old witch lying dead with the arrow through her heart. He saw a pitchfork she had dropped and flaming, red-hot fire coming out of its prongs. He knew the pitchfork was meant for him, but God saved the old minko that day. From then on, the place was called Devil's Den.

Jim swooped his arms in the air and flew around the girls while he told the story, like the owl.

"Papa Jim," Ella asked, "why would the bad men want to go to that scary place and hide?" She held her sister, who had kept her eyes closed with fright.

"Well, Ella, it has many boulders, and caves where bad men can make a fire and sleep warm at night. Many of them may not know the story I just told you. And so, my child, many may not have known a wicked witch lived there," he said.

"I want to go see Devil's Den." Ella jumped up to fly like Papa Jim.

"Not me," said Belle. "I don't want to ever see that place, Mama." She ran over to me.

"Not to worry," I said. "I don't think we'll be going near there. Papa Jim will let the constables and the sheriff go there and get the bad men. Then he'll put them in jail." I told the girls it was time for them to kiss Papa Jim good night.

Jim followed them into the new bedroom he'd built for them.

"Don't forget to have them say their prayers, Jim," I called from the end of the long room, warming my hands by the fireplace. We lived in much more comfort than I'd dreamed we would.

"Good night, Papa Jim," Ella reached to hug him.

Jim and I sat by the fire. "I love my evening time of stories with the girls," he said.

Inside I was thinking that tales of crime were not really ones I'd hoped he would share with them. Then I remembered Papa's stories of bravery and decided maybe Jim's were okay. Papa's stories made me a stronger woman, understanding there was both good and bad in our world and we were fighting to keep the good winning over the bad.

I asked, "Jim, have I told you about Papa's sad journey from his homeland in Tennessee when his people were forced to come to Indian Territory?"

"No, Esther. Please, tell me."

"Removal destroyed about half of Papa's people. They came

with only the clothes on their backs and what they could carry, no animals or plows.

"How were they going to till the land?" he asked.

"I do not know how they managed. They could only work the soil with sharpened sticks and if they got a plow and a horse, they would share it." I got up and stood closer to the fire. Jim wrapped his arms around my shoulders and we looked into the flickering flames together.

"Do not tell me anymore if this upsets you, Esther."

"I am just saddened by their hardships. But after Papa met and married Mama, he decided to bring her south, to where the Choctaws and Chickasaws settled. Mama was Choctaw."

"Yes, I remember." He continued to stoke the fire.

"Papa saw the Chickasaws and Choctaws as more willing to get along with the white men and the government," I said as I wrapped my shawl around me.

"You are lucky, Esther. Your papa was so knowledgeable," he said. "I'm hoping the legislature will create tougher laws. So many whites are coming in and marrying our Chickasaw daughters. Many men from Texas come here with cattle and want to marry because our daughters have land." He kept stoking the fire.

"But it's not just the white men that are doing wrong things," I said.

"I know. But in spite of all the constables and the lighthorse to keep us safe, whiskey might be our end." He sat back down in his rocking chair. "I do not think this drink called whiskey is going to help any of us catch or enforce any laws in our area." He rocked, in deep thought. "The white men sell it freely to our brothers," he said. "It's like they want us to get drunk and break their laws."

I had to agree. "You have enough to do to catch criminals. But now, you have to catch and jail all the drunks in town. We need to keep our girls from those people who want to bring harm to us. I will render a prayer to God to keep whiskey out of our town."

He chuckled. "Oh, you will? I am not sure you can handle a drunk man," he said with a stubborn grin.

He was starting to make me a little upset with him.

"Not to worry," he said, after noticing my expression. He took my hand. "I will protect you and the girls. I hope you never have to be confronted by a drunken man, ever, Esther. But I do believe you could handle most anything that needed to be taken care of." He smiled.

"Thank you, Jim Wolf," I said. "I was hoping you were thinking just that."

I think he was starting to understand the woman he married.

A GROWING FAMILY

One day, Jim got home a little early and met me at the barn door. "How was your day, Esther?" he asked.

"Just barn chores." I smiled and poked him with my broom.

"Well, I would imagine with all that is going on in the Chickasaw Nation, I was certain you would be reading," he said. The one little dimple in his cheek hinted at humor. I noticed in the sunlight the tiny flecks of gray in his beard.

"You know me, Jim. This morning I spent some time reading about reconstruction. Isn't that what the Chickasaw men called it? The reconstruction?" I asked.

He said it was and according to what he understood, it was a time when Chickasaws put a great deal of money and work into reorganizing the school system ruined by the Civil War. Besides reclaiming a dozen buildings as neighborhood schools, the Chickasaw Nation also undertook to repair and reopen its boarding schools, and work on them was just finishing.

"What do you think of them?" I asked, cautiously.

"I'm glad to see those old buildings finally put to good use. That way, criminals won't try to hide in them, anymore." He winked.

"Oh, you think they might?"

"I do." He nodded. "That's why Governor Overton signed a law establishing a female seminary at Bloomfield Academy. We run the school and it's well protected by the Chickasaw Nation." He raised his eyebrows. "I think it is time to send Ella and Belle there."

"Do you really think we should?" It pained me to not have my children near me and our culture. "Remember, Jim? That was where Nathan taught when he and Lottie were married. He came to our home to work with Ella and Belle's reading, even though time was scarce because he taught there, too."

"I have not seen him much since your sister died." He offered a sympathetic glance.

"I know. Since he married Tobitzy Humes, the girls have not seen much of their cousin Nelson. But I've spent lots of time with the girls, reading from the same Bible my papa taught me from. By the time Ella was ten, she was reading well from a fifth grader reader."

"Where is Nathan now?" he asked.

"I think he and Tobitzy are still in Tishomingo. But they have drifted away from us."

We decided to ask the headmaster for a paper to fill out so the girls could enter the school. Ella was now eleven and becoming quite a beautiful young lady, and Belle was just as polite and sweet, with as much charm as any eight-year-old. They were required to read well in the McGuffey's fifth-grade reader, like Nathan Price taught them from, as well as the New Testament.

"Oh, Mama, I can read all this easily," Ella said as she walked with Papa Jim into the Academy for enrollment.

"You are much too prideful, Little Eagle," I told her. "Your Mama is going to have to render prayers for you today."

I did not want to take her in. Jim was full-blood Chickasaw and people there knew him well. I felt a little out of place.

"You come with us, Esther," he offered.

"No. I am more in comfort letting you go. I reckon they should know I'm Indian, but many know I am not Chickasaw," I said. "I want no prejudice put upon my girls, on my account." I touched his hand. "I am fine with just you taking our girls."

I was told the purpose of Bloomfield Academy was to make sure our Indian girls would have "equal footing with our white brethren." But for me it was not about that. I wanted my girls to be better. I did not want the school to take away their feeling of family. They could speak Chickasaw and Choctaw, and even knew a few Cherokee words, but their English was even better. The academy was beautiful and welcoming, and looked like a very big home. I rendered a prayer the girls would love it there.

Although religion was very important in my family, it was also most important that they understood all about what was happening with our people. They were never to forget where they came from, their history and their elders. The girls did get to attend church services every Sunday and began each day by reading the scriptures. If the girls graduated, they could teach at any of the schools in the Chickasaw Nation.

Still, I had my reservations. "It is truly unfair to all of us that in order for our children to be educated they must attend boarding school," I told Jim.

"I know," he said. "I hate to have our girls be away from our family and away from our culture."

"I reckon it's more important that our girls be educated," I responded.

We agreed. Jim and I had high hopes for them.

That winter I began to feel sick again. I was thirty and had suffered enough tragedy to equal a woman of fifty, but I knew this sickness. It was morning sickness. Although I had grown to love Jim Wolf with all my heart, I was not sure how I felt about this pregnancy. In my experience, with pregnancy and children came the loss of a husband. I wanted so much to have a long life with Jim. He was a good man and father, and he shared our dream of having a son. I was reluctant to tell him at first. But I knew the time would come soon that he would notice.

It was a beautiful fall morning in Indian Territory. I felt the sun dropping its rich red color into the evening sky, shortening our days. I filled my life with sewing and with reading.

Another pain of loss had hit me hard that year. I lost my sweet Thunder. He was old and I hated to see him pass, but he'd been with me for almost twenty-five years. Not many I knew in any settlement around owned a horse for as long as I'd owned Thunder. I heard that old crow cawing at me the morning I walked into the barn to see Thunder lying in the hay. The air was dry and dust rose at my every step. My heart sank because I saw no movement, no whinnying, no hearing him bay. I knelt beside Thunder's still body, now without his spirit. It felt like I had lost another child. I knew I would never see him again in this world, but would meet him in a better one. I touched his soft face and told him, "We will ride fast, like the wind, again."

I wiped a tear away, as I reminisced his loss. Any loss was not easy for me, anymore. I felt tough in my skin, but too soft in my heart. Maybe it was being with child that made me so sensitive.

"What is my Esther going to do, today?" Jim asked as he crossed the room to grab his coat for work. His hand brushed my cheek, and felt the wetness of my face. "What's this, Esther? Have you been crying?"

"Oh, it is nothing," I said. "I was just remembering my Thunder this morning, and a sadness that the girls are off to school," I took the corner of my apron to dry the tears. "Not that I'm unhappy they were selected to attend such a wonderful school, but it will be so quiet for a little while. But maybe not for long." I turned and smiled, pointing at my stomach.

"What—oh, my, what?" he stuttered. "Is it true, Little Bird?" He only called me that when he was being particularly affectionate. He kissed my damp face. He spun me around with the turn of his hand.

"Oh, stop that, Jim Wolf. You are making me dizzy. Yes, Mr. Wolf, you are going to be a new father." I smiled.

"Are you sure?" he questioned, continuing with a little stomp dance of his own.

"Well, as sure as sure as I can be, being a woman who has had a few babies. So, I think I am either way too fat, or I am for sure going to have a baby sometime right before Christmas."

"Oh, my." He sank into a chair, dizzy from dancing around and not a little surprised at the news.

We embraced and he told me how honored he was to be having a child with me, his first, although he loved my girls as his own. We talked a few more minutes before he rushed out, realizing he would be late if he did not get moving.

Sometimes I found myself thinking of my first love, my Benjamin, when I was fourteen, and remembering how it felt to be so emotionally attached to someone. But when I felt the movement of Jim Wolf's baby, it was a new feeling—or maybe an old one I had not dreamed I could have again. It was those "God-like" responsibilities that come over you as a mother. Bearing a child at thirty would be different, and I was not sure who I wanted to use as a midwife. When I was younger, I never seemed to be worried about these things, but many life-changing events in the meantime had caused me to worry about how I might handle the birth. When cold weather set in, I knew Jim did not always get home before dark, and I would be alone.

I was once drawn to the idea I was my own best helper. I thought there really were no warriors or evil in this world. Since then my world had developed many warriors and many battles, and having a child was another step toward newness. I walked out and sat on the porch to look out at our land and render prayers of thanks for my blessings. How many fine men had crossed my path leaving me with my days in turmoil and danger, and I had come out okay? I thought of my brother, Rufus, and how I longed for him, his journey in life cut so short. I thought of my loss of Lottie and her last child. I remembered my first love, Benjamin, and my beautiful brave warrior husband, Houston. And I knew my people who had passed before me walked with me.

I became intrigued by the thought of becoming a mother again. I moved forward in my day, changing and rearranging the girls' room, and put on Jim's old straw hat to go to the barn to find where Houston stored Belle's crib. I found it there behind a pile of wood. It looked to be in bad shape. I moved the logs away from the crib, and something stirred, and scattering straw across my shoes. I heard a rustling noise and quickly looked down to see the coil of a tail rattling in the morning breeze. I had disturbed his resting place. The rattlesnake brought up his diamond-shaped head to face me.

I had learned from my papa to stay still. Any sudden movement could cause him to strike. His eyes, with their great poisonous slits, were open and wide. I reached carefully for Jim's hat and tossed it to my left. In the instant the rattlesnake lunged at my hat, I pulled my pistol from my apron pocket, and shot off the top of his head. I also put an enormous hole in Jim's old hat.

I watched his headless body slither through the straw on the floor for as long as it could, until I felt my baby kick, reminding me to breathe.

Breathe, Mama. Breathe.

I rendered a strong prayer of thankfulness.

"It is a good thing, Papa, you taught Little Bird how to use this gun," I said aloud.

The long sleeves of my dress and my apron shook. It was cold in the barn, but the shivers were from my near exposure to death. I slipped back toward the carcass, my gun in both hands. I had to make sure there were no others in the straw, waiting to take vengeance. I heard crows cawing on the fence outside. My fala, my "truth-talkers," were bearing down on me, telling me danger lurked. "Go away, fala," I called out. They were a little late with their warning, this time.

With my knife I cut off the rattle, evidence of my bravery. I carried the crib into the house and cleaned it up.

That evening Jim arrived home to hear the story of my bravery. He looked at the rattle resting on the table and told me how lucky I was. "It was a very large rattlesnake! I count fourteen buttons on his tail," he said.

I showed him his old hat with the big hole in it.

"Well, we will have to have a brave son, to help protect you when I am away," he said. "We will call him 'sinti ubi' which in Chickasaw means 'killer of snakes.'"

"I am thinking we are sure to have a brave daughter, like her mother." I picked up the hat and stuck my hand through the hole. "I was going to name her Harriet. And I think I will call her Hattie, which is a most appropriate name, don't you think?" I waved at him through the hole.

We laughed and held each other. I thought, this is a good man, my Jim Wolf.

GROWTH LEADS TO CHANGE

Jim hired a woman to stay with me, and Hattie was born shortly before Christmas in the winter of '85. Our Hattie had the most beautiful hazel eyes. My life was changing fast.

More wagons were on the roads, and more roads were built everywhere around us. The greatest problem was the growth of the white population. The irrepressible white man seemed to gain more power each year. Our men married white women, white men married Indian women, and all were adopted as Indian citizens.

"Things are really getting hard to manage with all the crime in Tishomingo," Jim shared one evening.

"What is going on?" I asked.

We had just put Hattie to bed, and sat talking by the light of the lantern. His face glowed when he shared his knowledge with me. I was proud of him.

"Big tracts of Indian lands are being leased to white men for them to graze and raise cattle," he said. "I know that is going to lead to change. How can we hold onto our settlements?"

"What do you mean, Jim?" I replied in panic. "How can the United States let that happen?"

"You knew the railroads were making shipping points for cattle," he said. "They are no longer driving the cattle to market. They ship them by railroad."

"That's just going to bring in more cattle rustlers and thieves, like the ones that killed my brother," I replied.

"Yes. And it's harder for us to put them all in jail," he admitted. He sighed. "Hogan and Sallie Maytubby have been our neighbors for over eight years. They just told me they sold their place. Said they were going to move into town, and sell all their cattle."

"Who bought their place?" I asked.

"A Chickasaw man named Holmes McLish. I know his brother, Richard. He's a lawyer for the Chickasaw Nation. Holmes and Richard own lands that stretch for more than forty miles."

"I knew them when they were little. Their papa used to bring them over to play when he came to visit my papa," I said. "Did he bring lots of cattle with him? I believe his papa was a big cattleman."

"Yes, and all of Maytubby's cattle, too," he said. "He's got land over by Reck with cattle on it."

"I thought most of the McLishes were around Ardmore? Why would he want to come all the way over here?" I wondered.

Jim shrugged. "They have more land than we'll ever see," he said. "But he should be a good neighbor to have."

I thought to myself about how Reck was not a territory my papa thought much of. He told me it was dangerous there, and the Comanche who lived near there were mostly fighters, and not easy to agree with. Jim leaned over to kiss me and put out the lantern, and we called it a night.

Ella was growing to be a beautiful young lady and Belle was right behind her. They came home for the summer, and were lots of help with Hattie. Mrs. Orr, the woman from Tishomingo who had helped with Hattie's birth, was an excellent midwife, but had to move back to town to work for a new doctor from Mississippi.

An Irish family moved onto a parcel of land north of Tishomingo. Their name was McSwain and they had two handsome, red-headed boys who took quite an interest in our girls. We often ran into them when we would go into Tishomingo. They spoke with their strange Irish brogue, which made the girls giggle and blush.

Two months after Hattie was born, I was pregnant again. The two younger girls would be just about a year older than each other. It would almost be like when Mama had us twins. I rendered a prayer to the Lord that the next child would be a little boy for Jim.

That next spring I delivered another girl, Mattie. She was precious and tiny, much smaller than Hattie. But now Hattie had a friend to play with. I worked most of the spring buying cloth and making dresses for them. My regular business of making cord for the mercantile did well. I felt glad my mama spent time teaching me how to sew, even if it took all her patience—much more than with Lottie. I always wanted to work outside with Papa and Rufus then. My life with four girls had certainly changed everything about me. I was getting good at making clothes and cords and making trades at the mercantile. Ella and Belle came home from boarding school to see their new little sister. Ella loved babies, and was excited to cradle and hold Mattie.

"Why don't you read to the girls?" I asked her.

She laid Mattie on a blanket and read from a book she'd brought home from school. The girls would look up at her with admiration as she moved around the floor when she read. She was never still. She was such a performer.

"Be still, my child," I reproved. "You have 'Chihowa lowak,' like your mother. Sit down to read to your sisters."

Ella sat to read more, but her arms still flapped like a bird's. She told me she was becoming quite a proficient speller at school.

"That is a big word, Ella. What does 'pro-fish-ant' mean"? I asked.

"It is 'proficient,' Mama. It means I am a good speller," she replied.

I am proud of her, I thought.

She told me they used Webster's Blue-Black Spelling book, and she could spell every word in it. She loved to have them test her, to prove she was good. Oh, her energy reminded me of myself at that age. I wanted to do things as close to correctly as I could.

"Mama, there is a spelling contest at school, and I want to enter it," she chattered away. She held Hattie's hand and played with her while she shared that excitement with me. Mattie was fully put off to sleep by her reading, and Belle lay beside Mattie on their blanket, looking totally bored with her sister's chatter.

"Well, I think that sounds wonderful, Ella," I said. "Would you like to practice some before you go back to boarding school this fall?"

"Oh, yes, Mama. I will go get the book now." She jumped up, and nearly knocked Hattie to the floor.

"Now, Ella, I did not mean this very moment." I moved Hattie away from Ella's bundle of energy. "There is a lot to do today. We have to go to Tishomingo to the see the new doctor."

I received a letter from one of Mama's cousins in northern part of the Territory, where they had suffered an outbreak of smallpox near Vinita, and along the Grand River. I asked Mrs. Orr about it before she left and she said I should see this new doctor, Trout.

"I was told that the new doctor is working to make the smallpox vaccination available that will keep you girls from getting sick," I explained to them.

"What is a vaccination, Mama?" Belle asked.

"It is where they stab you with something pointed," Ella blurted, poking Belle in the arm with her fingernail. Belle whined, and Hattie started to cry. I decided it was time to most dutifully send my very loud and smart little girl to sit, so as not wake Mattie.

"Ella, shame on you for making your sisters afraid." I brought Belle over next to me. She still trembled at the thought of a "big stick in her arm." Hattie was not helping. She pulled at Belle's hair.

"We don't know exactly how they do these vaccinations. I am sure that the new doctor is very kind, and will do them gently," I assured them. "And I don't know if they even have these vaccinations in Tishomingo yet, so stop worrying about something we know nothing about."

I did take them into Tishomingo the next day, and they were able to vaccinate all my children. Jim always seemed to trust my judgment with matters of the children, but it still made him a little nervous. He said he was glad to hear other families had done the same.

I was starting to feel sick again and I feared that something might be wrong. I asked the doctor if there was time to look at me. Running around the settlement, caring for the farm, and managing my four children was starting to take its toll.

"Dr. Trout, I have been feeling rather tired lately and not full of the energy I normally have," I told him after he took care of Hattie.

"Well, Mrs. Wolf, you have a three-year-old and a two-year-old to run after, so that should make anyone tired," he observed.

He still wanted to do a physical examination, and asked the woman helping him to take the children out of the room.

"Well...*Well*..." he said again, flustered. I was getting a little frustrated with him and his stammering. I blurted a few impatient words in Chickasaw.

"I need you to get it out. Tell me what is wrong with me."

I then realized he knew what I was saying. I had forgotten that some of our new doctors had made the effort to learn our language. I was duly embarrassed and rendered a silent prayer that the Lord would forgive me for my impoliteness.

"Mrs. Wolf, I am here to happily inform you that you are with child, again," Dr. Trout said, a broad smile beneath the facial hair most white men displayed in those days.

I was not excited to hear the news. I really did not want another baby. I had just recovered from the last two and had been sure my tiredness was from constantly running after them. However, my sadness passed quickly after I thought about how much I loved my children. Maybe this time I would finally have my warrior. And wouldn't Mr. Wolf be proud to have a son? Dr. Trout said the baby would most likely be here in the spring or early summer. I could not wait to get the girls into the wagon and tell them the news. It was a good day in Good Spring.

In May of 1888, I birthed my fifth daughter, Francis Wolf. If my first baby girl Jesse had lived, she would have been my sixth little girl. I guessed I was just not meant to have a son. However, she was our little warrior, with a head full of black hair, looking very much like her handsome Chickasaw father.

Ella and Belle came home from school that summer to help me with the three little girls. Ella was twelve and Belle ten, such lovely girls.

Ella became much involved with horses. She planned to breed her mare to one of the McLish's colts. Holmes McLish had been over twice to look at her horse and said it was fine-looking.

Ella also taught Hattie and Mattie to ride. I worried that they were too young, but remembered my papa had taught me when I was four.

It was a breezy summer day in Indian Territory when I decided to take Hattie and Mattie down to the Washita River to play on the rocks. Ella would help me, and Belle would stay home and watch Francis.

It had been years since I rode Thunder, who now raced somewhere in heaven. It was time my little girls got to enjoy some of the beautiful pleasures I did as a child. I hooked up Rufus's horse Feather, a small black and white, for Belle to ride.

"I will ride by myself on Blue," Hattie proclaimed. She had become quite skilled. Ella, who was quite a horse woman like me, had taught her well.

"I'll put Mattie behind me on my horse," Ella said.

I saddled up Butterfly, my new horse that Jim had bought for me. She was an older sorrel mare, beautiful, with an ever-flowing flaxen mane and tale. She had the same spirit as my soba, Thunder. "I packed a small lunch of dried beef, bread, and fresh blackberries I picked earlier this week," I said. "Does that sound good?"

"Yummy," Hattie responded, already pacing her horse around me.

We took our time at a slow walk, enjoying the Indian Paintbrush flowers scattered around. I wanted to just take the girls and run through the fields, but I wasn't sure where we could tie up Butterfly, who was too young and fresh. I could not be sure the mare would stay in one place, like Feather or Blue. I led the girls through the fields until my horse stopped just as we came into higher grasses, closer to the riverbank. I could smell the water. The moisture in the air smelled so fresh in the summer breeze. And there stood a beautiful patch of snakeroot.

"Oh, girls, look at the snakeroot," I said. "My papa used to pick it to numb wounds, like when we got a skinned knee, or if we needed to stitch a bad cut." I pulled a cloth sack out of my leather pouch. "Hold your horses still, girls, and let me get some of these roots." I dismounted Butterfly, sliding a rope around her neck to hold her steady. "We may need this snakeroot, someday, and it only comes at certain times of the year," I told the girls.

I filled the bag, and we rode on to the riverbank. I tied Butterfly to a tree and helped the younger girls off Feather and Blue. I told them to stay close, because the river was moving fast, lifting soft, foaming bubbles over the rocks. I did not want them to slip off the bank and tumble in.

We walked along, and the girls gathered a few stones. We sat under a tree and I taught them how to listen to the sounds of the water. We talked about listening to all the sounds around us. I told them they needed to learn to recognize the calls of birds.

"Look at the woodpecker in the tree next to us," I said. Then I pointed to a Red-tailed hawk in the sky, as it swerved downward to catch a rabbit.

"Oh, Mama, don't let that hawk get that rabbit," Ella cried. The hawk missed and flew away.

"Mama, look there." Ella pointed just above my head, at a low branch, where a black flicker of a bird flashed between the leafy limbs. Suddenly we heard cawing.

"It must be one of my followers," I laughed. The crow, far up on a high branch, was joined by two more. They all cawed noisily.

"What are those noisy birds?" Hattie asked, pointing at them. Mattie scurried behind me and grabbed my skirt.

"They are your mama's 'truth-talkers,'" Ella answered. "They follow and caw at Mama all the time. And they are most annoying. I wish I could shoot them."

"I am scared," Mattie muttered, still huddled behind me.

"They always seem to bring trouble," Ella grumbled, as if she was the authority on birds, like she was on spelling.

"Now, Ella, these fala are 'truth-talkers.' They often tell the truth to us when no one else will." I smiled at her, but frowned at them. I did not want the girls to fear them as I often did. Papa told me they were there to watch over me. But I had not seen the truths from these creatures to be anything but bad news. I waved my straw hat at them. They cawed and flew off to another tree. I had hoped we would have a quiet afternoon, without disturbances. I rendered a prayer that the crows would not visit me anymore to warn me of something bad happening. But as I thought that, the hair raised on my arms.

"Girls, let Mama teach you how to skip rocks," I gathered the little ones around me, and tried to shake off that feeling of unease.

"Oh, yes, Mama!" Ella exclaimed. "Let's skip rocks."

THE DOCTOR

I sat on the front porch early one evening in the year 1890, and watched Ella bring the cattle up. Darkness placed little shadows in front of each cow. I smiled as I watched Ella's horse work the cows and their shadows. J.D. McSwain and his brother, Charley, had come to the settlement a few times to show her and Belle how to work with cattle. Before Lottie died, she asked Nathan to split off forty head to our settlement, and Ella and Belle had a real chore to herd and work them. Ella especially found excitement running her horse and bringing up the herd.

Ella sold one of her horses to Holmes McLish, who had agreed to breed her mare to his colt. She had become a real hand at horses, so much that the McSwains would ask for her advice at training them.

"I love horses! I love helping with the cows," she declared one day to Jim and me.

"You are just like your mama," Jim remarked. "But I am not sure about you helping out those McSwains. They don't belong in Indian Territory!"

"She's better than her mama with horses," I put in, because she was. "Now, Jim, Ella has known J.D. McSwain a good while, and he seems to be a good Irish boy, even if he talks funny."

He raised his eyebrows. "I think my long working hours have kept me from noticing who Ella and Belle have been seeing."

Jim did work hard at keeping the doors of the capitol open for the Legislature, and his hours away from us had grown longer. I decided to enroll Hattie, Mattie and Francis in the Harley Institute, Belle and Ella were both falling in love with the McSwain boys. Our family was changing quickly. So were the times.

"What is happening with our town?" I asked Jim after getting home from a busy shopping day in Tishomingo.

"Well, after the land run that took the land west and north of us, I heard the president is opening up two million acres for settlement," he said. Frowning, he continued, "I am getting afraid for us, Little Bird. Render prayers that we can keep our settlement."

I cried myself to sleep that night. Papa had talked about this day coming.

The arguments were heard on every street corner in town. Our leaders would spend hours in court arguing they already knew which of their people belonged to their tribe, and that we did not need any council to determine for us who is Chickasaw and who is not. The Chickasaws did not seem worried about false claims from our new white neighbors.

Then Jim put his foot down. "I really don't want our girls seeing those Irish boys," he told me one night. He thought the McSwains only wanted to get more land by courting our girls. He did not see what I saw in my girls' eyes, two boys so handsome and charming. And I knew Ella and Belle would not listen to him.

"Those McSwain boys know a lot about raising big herds," I answered quietly. "Ella and Belle are fascinated by that."

"Well, I'm going to 'fascinate' them right out of my house if they come over here to see them," he grumbled.

"Now Jim, you have not met them, and you must judge people most respectfully," I said.

He raised an eyebrow, still not happy. "I'll show them respect. I just don't want them courting my girls."

It was not long after our conversation that Ella brought Joel Dayton McSwain to meet Jim, who actually liked him. I loved this man so, and he made me smile at the most unexpected times. In our eight years of marriage, I never saw him disrespect anyone.

The proposal came and Ella and J.D. made wedding plans. She had just turned sixteen. I was not happy with her getting married early in life, like I did. I had hoped she would have waited a little longer.

Jim came home early one wintry day in 1890. The wind blew little glistens of snow and ice along the corral fence while I put the last feed down in the stalls. I heard the three crows bellow at me and I hurried up to the house. I grabbed the reins to his horse as he slid down. He almost fell into my arms.

"What's wrong, Jim?" I helped him to the porch.

"My stomach hurts bad," he answered, tightly grabbing his right side. I made some light broth for him and helped him into bed.

"What do you think it is, Jim?" I pulled the covers up under his chin.

"Maybe I pulled something in my belly. It hurts low and deep. I was moving things around at the courthouse, probably lifted something I should not have." He moaned and rolled onto his side.

He spent most of the night in bed doubled up in pain. I tried to get him to drink some of the snakeroot broth I'd made. He agreed, after much resistance, but threw it all up. By the next morning, he seemed frail and weak.

"Jim, you're burning with fever," I said. I got one of the girls to bring cool rags for his forehead and prayed for him to heal quickly. All the girls were home for the Christmas holidays, so by mid-morning they helped me hitch the wagon and pack food for the trip to Ardmore. There was a new doctor there.

"Where are you taking me?" Jim asked. "I'll be fine," he whispered. "Please, Esther, just let me lie here and rest." He tried to look firm, but his face was pale and slack.

"I will not have you lay here in pain," I said. "I am taking you to the new doctor in Ardmore. Yarbrough is his name," I said. "He has helped a lot of people I know, and we are going to get you well."

Ella leaned over him, tears in her eyes. "Papa Jim, you have to see a doctor. A lot of people have been sick with some kind of influenza and we have to get you to a doctor. Please, Papa Jim. Please."

He nodded. Ella and Belle helped me get him to the wagon. J.D. McSwain came. I knew he was trying to win over Mr. Wolf's approval to marry Ella. J.D. helped me carry Jim to the back of the wagon and lay him across two quilts, each holding bright memories of my previous marriages. I covered him with a third, the wedding quilt Mama gave me to give to the first daughter who married. I hated the backs of wagons. They never gave me a good feeling. There were many bad memories in them. But it was the only way to get us safely there.

I loaded up the five girls, all in their finest church dresses. Waves of red and orange crested the skyline as we headed west. The sun was midway, so we had about a half a day or more to get to Ardmore. I rounded up the younger girls in the back with me and Jim. J.D. drove, with Ella and Belle up front.

Jim was still burning up with fever and I had brought damp cloths to keep his face cooled. I put a little of the snakeroot broth in the one of them and laid it on his side in hopes it would numb the pain. The three crows, silhouetted by their dark shadows, sat at the gate and turned their heads to follow us intently as we passed. Their black coats glistened tones of purple and dark red in the sunlight.

It was a long drive and it was late in the afternoon by the time we got to the doctor's office in Ardmore. Jim was still doubled up.

Dr. Yarbrough spoke kindly as he touched Jim's stomach and then motioned for J.D. to carry Jim into the examination room. He was too weak to walk, even with help.

"How long has he been like this, Mrs. Wolf?" he asked.

"Two days, now, but he got a lot worse on the ride over here. Maybe we should not have made the trip so far, with him this sick." Tears slid down my cheek.

"No, Mrs. Wolf, you did the right thing. But, I think he is going to need surgery," he said.

"Surgery? But why?"

He gently took my arm and led me away. "Please, would all of you wait outside in the waiting room while I finish the examination?"

"Yakoke," I said and gathered the girls and J.D. to my side to wait.

Soon he came back to ask J.D. to fetch his nurse, who had already left for the day. He asked if J.D. could ride a horse.

J.D. answered, "Aye, sir. I've been ridin' since me birth." The older girls giggled, but quickly stopped after a look at me. I did not allow any joy at this moment in my life.

"Sorry, Mama," they said.

While J.D. rode away, the doctor sat to tell me, "Mrs. Wolf,

I believe your husband has a ruptured appendix. It must be removed at once. I will prepare him for the surgery and wait for Mr. McSwain to return with my nurse. As soon as she arrives we will proceed. It is of utmost importance, Mrs. Wolf, that we get this surgery done as quickly as possible."

I shook my head, in shock, not really knowing what an appendix was. But if it needed to come out to make my Jim well, I knew it had better come out of there.

The doctor suggested we all move into his office where there was a rug and two big sofas. There the babies could nap while we waited. I was not sure how long the surgery would take, so I sent Ella out to the wagon to get the bag with bread and dried meat. Belle went out to bring in quilts for the babies.

J.D. soon returned with Miss McCoy, a lovely girl who did not look old enough to be a nurse. She had come with missionaries from North Carolina to work with Dr. Yarbrough, whom she knew from there.

I heard Jim wail. Miss McCoy rushed inside, where Dr. Yarbrough stood over Jim. The door closed.

We huddled together and said prayers, waiting for the door to open with news. It got dark outside before Dr. Yarbrough came out with his nurse. By a look at Nurse McCoy's face, I could tell the matter was serious. Dr. Yarbrough asked me to follow him out of the room. Nurse McCoy followed. I asked J.D. to stay there with the girls.

We walked back into the room where Jim lay on the table, his handsome face turned almost white-man pale. I ran to him and laid my head on his chest.

"I am sorry Mrs. Wolf," Dr. Yarbrough whispered. "We did all we could. The appendix has ruptured and the poison has spread all through his body. I don't believe he has much longer to live. I thought you'd better say your goodbyes now." He sighed. "Again,

Mrs. Wolf, I am so, so sorry."

"I am, too." Miss McCoy began to cry and rushed out.

I kept my head on Jim's chest and took his hand. His touch felt weak and limp, but I could feel a finger gently tap the top of my hand, in a most affectionate way.

"Please, Jim, don't leave me and the girls," I begged. "Please, dear God, heal my Jim!"

We held hands a few minutes longer. I wanted again to feel that gentle tap of his one finger. His hand slowly fell limp in mine and his eyelids fluttered a second, and he was gone.

"I want my 'Chihowa lowak,' back," I shouted. "I want what is mine back. Oh, he can't be gone! Please, not again!"

I held tight to his chest. Dr. Yarbrough gently took my shoulders and pulled me away.

I reached for him once more. Dr. Yarbrough told me he was gone, and drew the sheet over Jim's body. I looked at the contour of the man who meant so much to me. My heart was torn with pain.

Tears flooded my face, bursting as rain from a storm cloud. Images of my past swirled like a fast stomp dance. The swirl grew tighter and the dancers closed in, swallowing me in their middle.

I awoke on the couch in the doctor's office. Ella held a cloth to my forehead. All four faces of the rest of my brood lay on my chest and legs. Ella cried the most. Belle held Francis in her arms at my feet. I was wrapped in children, all crying for their loss as much as for mine.

The room was hazy. I saw Dr. Yarbrough speaking softly with J.D. I must pull myself together, I thought. Too many people were counting on me. I could not fall into a slump of pain like after Houston's death. Jim would not want me to. He was like Papa. He would want me to be brave. Jim would pull me up, straight up, and expect me to show courage. I slowly brought myself to sit up, bringing all the love of my girls into me, and we mourned together. I had loved and lost, so many times, and so had my children.

The doctor waited for us to wipe our faces. "Mrs. Wolf, I have made arrangements for the Methodist church to put you and your girls up for the night. They have a room at the church that you all can sleep in, and the women of the church will bring food over for you. Is that all right with you?"

He turned to J.D. "Son, you can leave your wagon and horses at my livery stable. I have an extra room for you."

We were taken to the church. I spent most of the night holding each of my girls as they cried themselves to sleep.

That morning the Methodist women came in to prepare some food for us to travel with. One brought a beautiful blanket to cover Jim's body. It was just more kindness than I could take at that moment. I excused myself and stepped outside, into the fresh morning air. I took several deep breaths. I could not ponder where fault might lie for Jim's death. "Oh, Lord, I got him here as quick as I could," I cried out to the sky. I reached up to make fists and shake them at the heavens, but stopped. "What are you doing, Esther Wolf?" I asked myself, aloud.

I knew God was not at fault, but I so wanted something or someone to blame. I lifted my apron and wiped the ugly, angry tears from my face. I looked around for those awful crows, but they were nowhere in sight. This would have been a perfect time to yell at them. Those three had followed me all my life, and now I had lost three wonderful husbands. I turned and walked back into the church and my children's arms, bravely.

Richard McLish came about mid-morning, and introduced himself as the Secretary of the Chickasaw Citizenship Commission. He said he would escort me back to Durwood with my girls and my wagon and Jim's body.

I stood to shake his hand. "I am Esther Wolf, Richard. I used to be Esther Wilson. My Papa Jesse knew your Papa when we were children."

"Of course, Mrs. Wolf—er, Esther. It has been a long time. So sorry for your loss." He tipped his hat in condolence.

"Your brother Holmes is our neighbor," I said.

"Holmes spoke highly of your husband," he said. "Jim was a fine National Jailer, ma'am. I know your girls were very proud of their father."

"I have been married going on almost nine years," I told him. "He was a wonderful husband and father. I don't know what I am going to do without him."

"The Chickasaw Nation wants an honorable burial for Mr. Wolf. I have been assigned to help you with anything you might need."

"Please meet Mr. McSwain. He drove us here," I said.

Mr. McLish helped J.D. load the wagon. He had brought another wagon to carry Jim's body home.

I rendered prayers all the way back to Durwood, holding my children close to me.

THE VISIT

The ride home from Ardmore felt arduous. J.D. was kind to drive us, for I knew I wasn't up to it. Richard McLish rode behind us in the wagon bearing Jim's body. I cried most of the way home, and so did the girls. I am not sure what they were thinking, but I wondered how I was going to manage them and my life at this point. Jim was our brave warrior, our friend, and the best father anyone could want.

When we arrived, we found a crowd at our house.

How did news travel so quickly?

Even the Reverend James Raper was there, with brethren from his church.

"We are so sorry for your loss," he told me. "You remember my wife, Mollie?"

"Yes, of course, I do. Good to see you, Mrs. Raper," I said. She handed me a basket of food from their church parishioners. "I remember you came when my brother Rufus died," I told her.

Holmes McLish walked into the house with J.D. "Chukma, Esther," he greeted me. "We'll take the horses to the livery."

"Yakoke," I thanked him.

Some men carried Jim into our bedroom, where people waited to prepare him for burial, along with Jim's coffin. The box was quite fancy. A member of the Chickasaw Legislature had made it. He'd carved the name, "WOLF," into its lid. I gave them the blanket the Methodist Church women of Ardmore had given me to wrap him in.

Weeks passed after Jim's funeral before I felt the need to go into town. The townspeople of Tishomingo had brought enough food to keep us for a month. All the same, I didn't wish to visit with anyone. Mourning my loss of Jim was a slow process. I wondered if it was because there had been so many losses, or because I was not as brave as Papa expected me to be. I knew only one thing, that my five girls needed me to provide a good life for them. I felt surrounded by the spirit of my culture. I had to be braver than ever before.

Ella and I loaded Hattie, Mattie, and Francis into the wagon. It was a day of happiness for Ella. I had to buy things to prepare for her wedding to Joel Dayton McSwain. She was ready to have her own place and children, and was so much like me that I feared for her. But I lifted my heart to the sky, and prayed for her happiness. It was late November. The fall air already was bitter, foretelling a cold winter, so I had to buy cloth for her dress, and the dresses for the three little ones. Belle was to meet us in town later. She had gone to meet her teacher to get assignments before graduation.

When we arrived in town, a Chickasaw woman, Mary Roberts, stopped me on the walkway to the mercantile. "How are you, Mrs. Wolf, and your lovely girls?" she asked.

"Yakoke, Mrs. Roberts, we are just fine," I replied.

"Have you heard what happened to the lawyer, Mr. Richard McLish?"

I said I had not, and of course, she proceeded to tell me. "A shooting affray took place at the residence of a Mr. Watkins in Ardmore," she whispered.

"What happened?" I questioned softly, and leaned in closer. The little ones leaned in, too. I was hoping they had not heard much.

"May I be excused, Mama?" Ella interrupted politely.

"Yes, dear, go on into the mercantile and I will be in shortly," I said and gave her a nod.

"Nice to see you, Mrs. Roberts," Ella said.

"Yes, dear, you, too," Mrs. Roberts said, and pulled me closer. "Well, three men nearly escaped death! It was Bill Watkins and his brother Bob, and Mr. McLish."

"I like Mr. Richard McLish, a most honorable man. He was so helpful to us when my Jim died," I said, hoping to keep her story on the lighter side of things.

Mrs. Roberts stepped up on the boardwalk so we could sit on a bench in front of the mercantile.

"Well, Bill Watkins is an Indian by marriage, and you know, Mr. McLish is Chickasaw, and they got into an argument about the land that they each claimed, which you know is the biggest part of the town of Ardmore." Mrs. Roberts continued. She picked up Mattie and sat her in her lap.

"What happened?" I wanted her to finish the story. Mattie played with the ruffles on Mrs. Roberts's apron. I hoped she was not listening.

"While they argued," she continued, "an eyewitness said Mr. McLish did not threaten or use loud language, but in a moment, Mr. Bill Watkins pulled a gun and fired twice at him, neither shot taking effect." She laid her hand over her mouth, as if telling a horrific story.

Both the girls' eyes got big. At that moment I couldn't really move them off the bench, so I just waited for her to finish.

"And then, and *then*," she said, sighing deeply, "all of a sudden, Bill's brother Bob came running, with his gun pointed at Mr. McLish." She again gasped. All my girls' eyes got big again. Mattie moved over to my lap with Francis. Hattie skipped around busily on the boardwalk.

"What did Mr. Richard McLish do?" I asked. I had a handful, so Mrs. Roberts took Francis.

"Mr. McLish drew his six-shooter, and fired three shots, two effecting on Bill, and one on Bob. Bob was struck in the arm, and Bill was struck in the shoulder," she exclaimed. "I guess all the parties meant business."

"Oh, my," I said. "What happened to Mr. McLish?"

"I heard the Indian court found in favor of him," she said. "And I was not surprised by that, at all." She wiped her forehead, as if there was perspiration there to wipe on such a cool day.

"Thank goodness Mr. McLish was treated fairly," I said. I thanked her for her information and decided it best that the girls and I stop by the settlement of Holmes McLish on our way home and offer our concern for his brother.

Belle came running down the boardwalk to hug me and her sisters. We walked into the mercantile and I visited with the clerk, Mr. Hindemon Burris. Frank Byrd, the postmaster in Tishomingo and brother of Governor Byrd, owned the store with Mr. Burris. Mr. Burris, an auditor for the Chickasaw Nation whom we had known a long time, offered his condolences for the loss of my Jim and congratulated me on the upcoming wedding of my eldest. He offered Burris Chapel, the church just outside Tishomingo he'd built in his father's name, for the wedding, and showed us some beautiful material for Ella's dress.

We found the best of cloth in white for Ella's wedding dress, and the girls picked out material for their dresses. We stepped outside. Belle noticed some men moving a large bell away from the capitol building.

"What is happening with the bell over at the capitol?" she asked. She was always fascinated by bells, after I told her the story about her name.

"Chikasha intulli ola—the Chickasaw capitol bell," I told her. "It used to be at the old Chickasaw capitol building, but I heard it was going to be moved."

"What is it used for, Mama?" she asked.

"It was used to summon tribal members to special meetings and for emergencies in town. Depending on the type of ring, our people would know whether it was a meeting or a death. They would come to the capitol to find out. Sometimes they would hear vital information that affected their lives," I explained as we continued to walk towards our wagon.

Four men balanced it precariously on a long wagon with small wheels. The bell was about two feet tall, and must have weighed as much as two large men. They would take it to the stump of the big bois d'arc tree next to the capitol.

We loaded up our wagon and headed for Durwood. On the way we passed by Holmes McLish's place. We found him working with a calf near the roadway. It looked like the calf was down and, of course, the girls wanted to stop to see what was going on.

"Chukma, Mr. McLish," I called to him. He tipped his hat, but could not move from the calf, upon which he had quite a grip.

Ella jumped down from the wagon to help. "Mr. McLish, what is wrong with the calf?"

"It has a sore hoof, and I am trying to examine it," said Mr. McLish.

"I am good with animals, sir," Ella said. "May I hold the calf for you?"

"Yakoke." Mr. McLish gingerly transferred one front hoof and one back hoof to Ella. She grabbed both and sat with the calf's back under her knees, holding it as strongly as any man could. She really did know what she was doing. Mr. McLish bent and pulled an arrowhead out of the calf's injured hoof. He took a rag from his back pocket and tied it around the hoof to stop the bleeding.

"How did the calf get that arrowhead in his hoof?" Ella asked, over the calf's loud bawls of pain.

"Oh, my son Willie was practicing with his bow, and he accidentally shot it. The shaft broke off when the calf ran away, and I have been trying to catch it for two days to get the arrow out," he explained. "Thanks, *Ososhi*," he said referring to Ella by her nickname, Little Eagle, in Chickasaw. She looked surprised, and he smiled. "I heard from others in town that they call you that. It fits you well."

"And how are you, Mrs. Wolf," he asked.

"I am well, Holmes. And please, call me Esther," I said. "I was wondering how your brother Richard was doing. I heard there was some trouble over Ardmore way."

"The trouble was easily resolved," he said vaguely. I sensed he did not wish to discuss the topic any further.

He nodded to Ella that it was okay to let the calf run free. The calf kicked up its hind legs like nothing was wrong, and ran off to find its mama.

"We'd best be going, Holmes," I said. I beckoned to Ella to board the wagon.

"Thanks for stopping by," he said, with a slight tip of his hat, again. "Travel safe, and nice to see you again, Mrs. Wolf—uh, I mean Esther," he said. "I will tell my brother you asked of him."

"Chipisalacho, Holmes McLish," I said, bidding him farewell. All the girls giggled and waved goodbye.

THE ENUMERATORS

The Five Civilized Tribes took a census in 1890. The idea, we were told, was to find and root out squatters. The tribes sent out what they called "enumerators," mostly Indians like us, and the lighthorse police to help them find people. But they always seemed to miss at least one member of this or that family. And we couldn't feel comfortable with the way they kept coming back and asking different questions, without ever explaining why.

"I hate those enumerators," Ella complained. "They keep coming by and not counting me as Chickasaw, and my papas were both full-blood Chickasaw."

I had to admit my Papa would have been upset at the way the enumerators took their information. He would have said that they were careless in their ways.

"They asked me if I was Indian," she added, shocked. "What kind of question is that, Mama?" She stomped her foot. "Why didn't they ask me my tribe? Why didn't they ask me who my papa was?" She fumed. "This is why the Chickasaws want a census based on our families only, and only those from Indian families. It's like these enumerators don't want to listen to us."

I tried to placate her. "Well, Ella," I said, "it is like what Papa Jim always told us. So many of us are intermarried now."

"I know, Mama. But Papa Jim liked J.D.," she said. She teared up.

I took her hand. "He loved J.D. and he saw how J.D. helped him when he got so sick. He's not the problem. The problem is so many who claim to be Indian even if no tribe says so. And the tribal elders are getting frustrated about it," I added.

"They're having a meeting this week," she said. "I wish we could go and be 'a mouse in the corner' to hear what they say," she said.

"Oh, you are definitely my child," I chuckled and gave her a hug.

By then we were wearing clothes that made us look more like white women. The enumerators looked like white men, too. Many Chickasaw women still wore moccasins and shawls. Things were changing around us, but we never gave up our stomp dances or our games of stickball.

Now whiskey had been brought into Indian Territory by the white men. The spirits were not supposed to be sold here. Most of the distilleries were found in the Ozark mountains of Arkansas. But more and more, they were found right here in Indian Territory.

Once I walked Mattie and Hattie to the back of the settlement, looking for wild blackberries. That's when I found vats and signs that someone had been going back there to make whiskey. I rushed the girls back to the house and told Belle to watch them while I went to shoot a wild turkey I thought I'd seen. I did not want to tell them the truth. It would have been dangerous for them to know what was really back there.

I took Jim's old rifle and returned, quietly and carefully, to the spot. I hoped no one would be there. I saw a turkey but did not shoot for fear of alerting someone. When I got to the still, I shot holes in everything and battered it with all my might. Whoever came back there would think a man had done it, which was fine with me. I did not want anything to do with this drink that altered men's thinking and created violence. It smelled strange, and I saw wisps of smoke rising from it. I grabbed a pan and went to the creek to get some water to douse it.

Suddenly, I heard men's voices behind me. I quietly hid behind a tree, the rifle in my hands. I could not see their faces, but I could tell there were three, all white men, talking very fast. One yelled something about everything being shot up. I eased away and then ran like a deer back through the woods back to my home. After I put the girls to bed, I sat with my rifle quietly by the door until my eyes finally closed, afraid those men might come hunting for the perpetrator. When sunlight first showed through the cracks in the slats of my home, I looked for signs of anyone near our house. There was none. I hoped those men decided to move their "spirit making" elsewhere.

After Ella married and moved to the McSwain family settlement, Belle and Charley McSwain decided to start planning their wedding. Of course, Ella was right in the middle of that. She loved to be involved. I wasn't sure, with all her chores, that she could come help me with her little sisters, but I knew she would make a wonderful mother. She was also such a hand with the horses and the cattle. I always thought cattle were strange creatures. They always seemed to have a leader cow that kept them going in the same direction, all in a line, at feeding time.

My comfortable life was not so comfortable anymore. That first winter was hard without any man to help me. Jim had spent time before he passed redoing the house and the barn. He covered the barn with clapboards made of oak blocks he'd split by hand, making it much warmer on cold winter days while I fed the stock. We had three hogs left and I had them butchered in Tishomingo to give us meat to live off of. I remembered when Rufus and I would hunt deer. I rarely had time in my days for hunting now, though I did take the girls turkey hunting and we came back with plenty for the holidays. The fishing, however, was not good that year.

We celebrated Christmas alone. Ella and Belle celebrated with the McSwains and neither could get a covered wagon to come over to our place. Besides, it had snowed, and I did not want the girls to travel in that kind of weather. The winter was awfully hard, but Papa had taught me how to cure meat from the turkeys and the hogs in our fireplace, so we had that and plenty of cornbread and biscuits.

But winter ended quickly, and spring came early. We needed to plant crops for ourselves and for our cows. Our two plows, one twelve-inch and one fourteen-inch, were more than I could handle by myself. We tried to plant corn, but I needed someone stronger to work the plows. I decided it might be a good time to ride over to Holmes's settlement and see if he could spare any help. I could only afford part-timers. I also needed to get out of the house. It had been almost two years since I'd lost my Jim.

The girls and I mounted the wagon for a beautiful afternoon ride. The fala were perched up in a tree, branches budding around them. They watched as we left the settlement and headed down the road towards the McLish place. I could hear them caw at me, their sleek black feathers glowing in the sun. The biggest one's eyes followed us down the road. The other two just cawed at each other. I was surprised to see them that morning. They had been away for quite a while.

"Good afternoon, Holmes," I hailed him and his son, Willie.

I wasn't sure if Willie was there all the time. It was my understanding that Holmes had been divorced. But he seemed to be a good father. Hindemon Burris and his wife, Viola, were there, about to mount their wagon and leave. I had not realized their friendship with Holmes. Mr. Burris tipped his hat and took his wagon out of my way.

"Sorry to bother you, "I apologized. "Please, tell your friends not to leave. I can only stay a minute."

He shook his head. "They were on their way to a meeting in Tishomingo," he explained.

"Well, Holmes," I said, getting down to business, "I am looking to hire some help on the ranch, and wondering if you could spare any part-timers in need of more work?"

Holmes asked Willie to take my horse and wagon and offered a hand for me to climb down. "Yakoke," I said to Willie, and told the girls to stay in the wagon. They giggled at him. I turned to Holmes for his response to my question.

"It seems to me, Esther, that it has been a long time since you have come to ask for any help," he noted. "I thought often that I should go over and check on you and your girls. How have you managed this last cold winter all by yourself?"

I raised a curious brow at his question. "Well, I have two new sons-in-law who have been most helpful, but they are planning families of their own right now. So, the girls and I are looking to hire some help."

"I had been hoping you might come over and ask for my help long before now, but I am grateful you finally did." He smiled briefly. "What kind of help do you need over in Durwood?'

"Mainly with the cattle and also some plowing," I said. He was a rather curious man, I thought. He'd been married several times, and I believe he thought highly of himself. He was tall and thin, and quite handsome.

"Well, I am sure we have some who would come and do just that. May I suggest that I come over and assess your needs?" he asked. "That way I could better choose the right man to send over to help." He sounded very business-like.

"Well, of course, I would love for you to stay for lunch." I started walking back toward my horse and wagon, and the girls. "Would tomorrow work for you, Holmes?"

"Why, yes it would, Esther," he said. He followed me and gave me a hand up to my wagon. He tipped his hat to the girls, and said, "Chukma."

The girls giggled like they had done with Willie. *They are such silly girls, but they are mine.* I drove away thinking he had been somewhat friendlier than I remembered him from before. He was kind of an odd man, but I did like him. I was not sure about another man in my life, especially one who had been divorced. I had far too much tragedy in my life and I was ready for peace and quiet. Having three young girls to raise by myself was not something I looked forward to, but I knew I could do it. I was not an old woman and I wondered what God planned for me.

I rode away actually looking forward to lunch the next day with Holmes. I was on a mission to make sure my children got all they deserved and living for the moment that my life would offer some reason for all my tragedy. I rendered a prayer as I rode through the gate, past the fala waiting to greet their Little Bird.

SO MANY LOVES

In the year 1893, I headed into a new relationship. It had been almost three years to the day of my Jim Wolf's death. I am not sure I was ready for marriage again. Still, I had found a simple court-ship from a wonderful, charming Chickasaw man—my neighbor, Holmes McLish. We courted for almost a year before he asked to marry me. I knew of his previous marriages and I saw little of his son, since Willie was off and married by then.

Security was an important reason why I accepted Holmes's request. Everywhere around us was turning more violent than before, especially in Tishomingo. I felt safer having a man about the settlement.

Hindemon Burris took Holmes into town to help him find a wedding outfit. It was May 1893, and I had a hunch the Indian Territory summer was going to be an especially hot one. Hinde-mon's wife, Viola, helped me measure and fit a wedding dress, one fancier than I ever worn before. I planned on wearing it with my mother's wedding shawl.

All three girls, Hattie, Mattie and Francis, were excited. I am not sure the older girls were that happy about my marriage to Holmes. Ella stopped coming by once she heard of my intent to marry him. She and Belle had heard rumors about his other marriages, which were never good. I was disappointed they weren't more supportive. However, Ella lived about eight miles away and Belle, about ten miles, both were grown women, and they were busy with their own lives. Since they were married to their Irish McSwain brothers, I figured they should be less interested in what their Mama was doing.

Ella also didn't like that Holmes pastured some of his cattle over in Reck. "Mama," she told me once when I chanced upon her in Tishomingo, "It is not safe there. I don't want you going there with him."

I already knew she didn't want me to go and why. I'd told her too many stories Papa shared with me and I'm sure she believed all of them. Holmes said they were all rumors, mostly because of cattle rustlers over that way and deals gone bad with white cattle buyers, now and then. But I would not have gone to Reck, anyway. Papa made a believer out of me and my girls reminded me often about that.

We planned to be married in late May at the same place Ella had her wedding. Hindemon Burris's father, Colbert Burris, was going to marry us. I mostly looked forward to my new life with Holmes, but I struggled with uncertainty after some very strange dreams. In them the fala were hanging around the fence line again, looking like the same three old birds, the biggest sporting his authority over the other two. You would have thought that at least one of them would have come upon some kind of accidental death or ill fate by then, but they were all still there, still following me. But whether they were the same three, I was sure I would never know in this lifetime.

The wedding was beautiful, but sad because my two older girls were not there. I knew it must have had to do with Holmes and Hindemon raising cattle like the McSwains did. I was never certain there was any kind of rivalry and Holmes never mentioned a word against them. I hoped Ella and Belle felt it best to stay away because they feared a disagreement, and did not want anything to ruin my wedding day. For their part, I certainly never heard them say one bad thing about Holmes, either. It seemed to me the tone of the day was more about rivalry between successful Indians and successful white men. I was not sure I liked the direction we were going, but I knew one thing for sure. Progress had come to Tishomingo. The wedding was quite nice, in spite of them not being there.

I spent the first three months of my marriage realizing my husband traveled more than I wanted him to be gone. It wasn't that he would not ask me to go with him—he did. But I still did not want to go anywhere near Reck. He worked over there with a man named Roff, who owned a big acreage with great herds of cattle next to where Holmes's herds were pastured. Holmes told me he decided to move to Durwood, so he would be nearer to the Chickasaw capitol, and because the trade was better there for his stock. But he would be gone sometimes as much as three weeks. We wrote letters to each other, and they kept my heart warm when he was not with me. He hired several men to work the settlement, so I was never left without help.

After the land runs of 1890, the dreams of most cattlemen around us became improbable, and staying self-sufficient by cattle ranching was a constant struggle. Holmes talked often with me about those dreams. He was quite a dreamer.

"For me to truly operate my cattle business, all white men need to be banned from Indian Territory," he told me frankly.

"I don't think that will ever happen, Holmes," I said.

"You're right. It's just a pipe dream," he admitted. "We can't even collect taxes from the white men who graze on our land. Our dreams won't ever happen," he said.

I responded, "I understand. Jim used to tell me the Chickasaws could not enforce the taxes due from the white men. The white ranchers just wanted to manipulate tribal laws to their benefit and often did so by pitting one tribe against another."

Holmes was good at earning money, but the cattle operations he ran in two places meant more time away from home. I knew my eldest daughters were caught in the middle of discussions about white men's cattle, and that was why they still did not come around much. I think Holmes felt the McSwains just wanted to acquire more Indian land. I understood why the girls tried to avoid any confrontation Holmes might have with J.D. or Charley McSwain. Any discussion could have become heated. I personally saw the McSwains as good men, living in a new land, just like us.

I was proud of my girls, though. They were successful and happy. Ella finally came to visit me and the girls, and brought my little grandson, Harry. He had a headful of curly black hair and was such a handsome boy. I knew Ella was proud to have a son. She seemed to get along with Holmes just fine. After all, he often praised her skills at handling horses and cattle.

I found out early in our marriage I was pregnant again. I was not sure Holmes was thrilled about it like my other husbands were. He was a man of business and already had a son. His time away from home made it difficult for me to find happiness in carrying his baby. But he was a good man to me and I knew this child would be loved. Hattie, Mattie, and Francis were fully counting on a little sister. I had not shared my news with Ella, who was also pregnant again with her second. I was going to be a grandmother for the second time and a mother again, all in the same year. I was thirty-eight, with five girls and one on the way, and a grandson to boot. I was starting to feel very old.

Holmes left to go to Reck the morning I told him I was pregnant. He told me some cattle were stolen off our place, about fifty head, and he had reported it to the sheriff earlier in the week. His foreman had gone out to get an official count of the stock.

"Why do you have to leave for Reck?" I asked.

"I think I may know who stole some of our cattle," he answered with a frown. "On my way to Reck, I'm going to stop off at Willie's place because he knows who it might be. If I find the cattle, I am going to need cash to pay someone to herd them back here," he said. "Have you picked up our annuity check yet?" he asked.

"I did. I bought some staples with it on the way home yesterday," I said. "I have seventy-two dollars left." I pulled the cash from my apron pocket.

He counted back twenty to me. "Fifty dollars ought to be enough to pay someone to help me herd those cows back here if I can find them. I hate it, but most of the herd that was stolen were those you'd brought to our marriage, Esther." He reached for my hand.

"They'd still have the brand 'Z' on them, so they should be easy to spot," I reminded him. "Be careful, Holmes," I said. "I hope you have safe travels and I love you." I squeezed his hand.

He kissed me and patted my belly and smiled. "Not to worry, Esther. I am happy that we are having a child together." He winked at me as he left. *Such a handsome and considerate man*, I thought, as I watched him ride off.

A week went by and the girls and I kept busy getting the baby's room ready. I already started a new quilt. The girls were excited to start school at the Harley Institute and we had lots of things to do.

Three days later, a rider brought me a letter from Holmes.

My dear Esther,

I have made it safely to Reck and on the way, I met a man who will help me get the cattle back. I will be back the end of next week. Willie gave me the name of the man that is said to have some cattle branded with the letter 'Z.' I will try to get the sheriff to go with me and help me talk to the thief. If not, I will come back without them. I will stop off at Joe Bynum's for one night on my way back. It may be dark when I get home.

Missing you,
Holmes

I appreciated Holmes's letters. He was a considerate man, and I believed he sincerely wanted our child. I felt happy.

Five more days passed with no sign of Holmes. I did not sleep most nights. The baby was starting to move a lot, and sometimes I just got up and did chores because I could not sleep. On the sixth night there came a knock at the door, long before daylight.

It was Ella and Belle, bursting through my doorway, in tears.

"Shh, child, y'all are going to wake the girls." But Ella was sobbing and carrying her son, little Harry, in her arms. Belle was hysterical.

Ella said, "Mama, J.D. came with us. He is outside tying up our horses."

"What's the matter?" I asked. "Will someone tell me what is going on?" I said firmly, "Tell Mama, please."

J.D. came in before they could say anything. And then, in walked a Chickasaw constable.

I decided to sit down. My house was full of people and I still did not know why.

Ella and Belle came and sat close to me.

"Mrs. McLish, I am Constable McGill. Your husband Holmes has been killed," he said, so matter-of-factly.

"Oh, my sweet Lord, this cannot be true." I fell into Belle's arms. "That just cannot be true, Constable. Please tell me it isn't so." I held Belle's hands in mine. "I just got a letter. My Holmes is on his way home from Reck," I shook a finger at the constable. Belle grabbed my hand and put it back in my lap. "You must be mistaken," I snarled, shaking my head at him.

"No, Mama. It is true," Ella said. She wrapped her arms around Belle and me.

J.D. looked at Belle and me, and tried to explain. "Nana, 'tis was an accident. Please know 'dat, Nana," he said in that beautiful Irish accent. He touched my shoulder. His voice cracked and he was almost in tears. He sounded upset, just repeating himself. "I am so wit' grief 'fahr you, dear Nana," he said and turned away.

And it all hit me. They were telling me the truth. I hurt all over, and truly felt like I was going to throw up. I left and Ella followed me into the bedroom.

"Mama, do you want a drink of water? What can I get you, Mama?" She held me close. "I am sorry, Mama. I know you thought that I did not like Holmes. I really did. I just did not want you to marry again and be hurt again." She cried. "Oh, Mama, it is happening to you again. I am so sorry, Mama, it just can't be happening to you again!" she sobbed. "It's not fair, Mama. It is just not fair!" She hugged me tighter.

"It's okay, Ella. Just give your Mama a moment," I said, my face wet with tears. I dropped to my knees and started to pray. Belle came into the room and knelt. "Mama, they took Charley away," she stammered. "Mama, I am pregnant, and they took my Charley away."

She fainted.

Ella and I caught her and called for J.D. to get a wet rag. Belle started to come back awake.

"Oh, Belle, you scared me, my child." I wiped the cool cloth across her face. "Let's get her to my bed." Ella and J.D. helped me get her to the bed and now we heard the cries of a child from the other room.

Ella went out to find Constable McGill comforting little Harry, who was crying in the corner of the kitchen.

Our world was turning upside down again, and what was I to do? I did not even realize Harry walked into the room, what with all the chaos. I had to be brave. That is my culture. That is my way. That is what Papa taught me.

I asked Constable McGill to please sit back down at the table. I took Harry into my lap and held him while Ella went back to be with Belle. There were three pregnant women in this house, all in terrible emotional pain. I touched my stomach, letting the unborn child know I was still there and would always love and care for them. I took a huge, deep breath and turned to the constable.

"Where is my husband?" I asked him.

He told me they took Holmes to Tishomingo because his death was a crime, and a coroner had to look at him. He had died instantly, after being shot twice in the back. And he told me who shot him.

"Oh, Aba Binili." *Lord, I pray for this constable.* This man had no idea how to speak to people. He was the most direct person I have ever met. What he had said certainly did play out in my mind. I could see flashes of fire and bullets in the dark. The images were vivid, in painful color. I wiped my face with the apron and hugged Harry, shaking. I rocked him back and forth for a minute. I looked around the room, at this place of great sorrow, and at the constable.

"Thank you for coming," I told him, my voice shaking. "Could you please give us time to process all this? We will all come back in the morning," I promised.

"I am happy to give you some time, Mrs. McLish. I am sorry for your loss." He still was abrupt, though. "You will need to come into Tishomingo first thing in the morning."

I nodded, thanked him and closed the door behind him.

Now I had to figure out what to do next.

THE ARDMORE TRIAL (1902)

The Dawes commissioners filed back into the room, past the doorway where Ella, Harry, little Holmes, and I had shared a lunch of biscuits and pork, packed in a bag along with my paperwork. I had brought letters from neighbors of my settlement stating that I was a woman of good standing and kindness, and a good mother to my children.

The October breeze picked up and I knew that it was a day in Indian Territory that prophesied colder weather to come. I took an old shawl from my bag to wrap around Holmes and Harry, kissed them softly, and asked them to sit quietly. I hoped it would not be much longer. We knew it was going to be a tiring wagon ride home.

The man with the ancient voice asked me to step back into the room. I was supposed to sit my body in front of them. The chair had gotten bigger than I remembered earlier and the room smaller. I hoped to be the strong woman I planned to be that day. I knew the questioning was about to get tougher and more brutal.

Mr. Murray pulled at the bottom of his beard to smooth it and opened with, "Where was Holmes McLish when he was killed?"

I told him he was killed four miles from Tishomingo. "I was not near the place where he was killed," I added. He was getting bolder in his questioning. I felt the hair raise on the back of my neck. I hoped I would not get flustered again.

He asked, one shaggy eyebrow raised, "You say you and Holmes McLish lived together without any separation until his death?"

"No, sir. You changed my words. I would not go out west to Reck. That means we were only apart when he was gone to Reck."

Mr. Murray saw I was getting a little upset. He lowered his voice. "So, he went off to the western part of the Chickasaw Nation?" he asked.

Again, I told him that Holmes would go out to Reck to check on his cattle, but that I would not go out there with him.

"How long would Holmes stay out in Reck?"

I thought about my answer, then carefully said, "He would stay sometimes four or five weeks, come back home, and then he would go back out to Reck again. But I would not go out there." And my statement was firm.

Then the big question came out, which I fully expected. Mr. Murray asked, "Did you ever have anything to do with any other man while he was away?"

I answered forcefully, "No, sir. If I did, I would say so. I have nothing to hide."

Two commissioners turned to each other to whisper, and handed Mr. Murray a handwritten note. Mr. Murray read it, placed his finger on a spot in the paper, and folded his arms. He raised his voice again. "Is it not a fact that there was some trouble between Holmes McLish and the McSwain boys at the time

Holmes McLish was killed?"

I responded flippantly, "No, there was no trouble!" I sat up, rod-straight, and braced for the next round. I whispered, "Ikim-ilho." Be brave. My previous husband Jim Wolf, the Lord rest his soul, often said it to me.

Mr. Murray began again, "Were not the McSwain boys well known to you?"

I said, "Why, of course! They are my sons-in-law."

He interrupted with, "Was that your daughter—one of them that was back here, just now?"

"Yes, sir."

"Is that the only daughter of yours that married a McSwain?"

As the entire commission looked on, I explained, "Two of my daughters each married a McSwain brother. And I never knew of any trouble between the McSwain boys and my husband."

Mr. Murray returned to his seat and passed a paper down the table to another commissioner, who looked down at it, and then up at me. "Did you ever find out who killed Holmes McLish?" he asked.

I hesitated, reluctant to answer, because I knew my life would never be the same if I did. I had to tell the truth, though.

The commissioner handed the paper back to Mr. Murray, who wiped a hand across his lips.

"Yes, sir," I said.

My mind flowed back to that evening.

My pain felt huge.

I heard the voices clearly ...

"And where is my son-in-law, Charley McSwain?" I asked Constable McGill. I had to, after hearing what Belle said before she fainted.

"They have taken him to jail, Mrs. McLish," he said. "He admitted to the crime and said he was shot at first, and that it was dark

and he did not see who it was, but thought he was shooting at a cattle rustler. Mr. McSwain claimed it was an accident."

I shook myself of my drifting thoughts, and came back to the present. I answered the commissioner, plain and simple. I told him the man was my son-in-law and that he did kill Holmes. I added, quickly, "If Charley says it was an accident, then it was an accident."

Mr. Murray asked if he was taken up for killing Holmes McLish and convicted for it.

My mind fell again back into the space of the pain in my past. I knew they were going to get to this. My daughters had married some fine Irish ranchers who had bought settlements around us and owned lots of cattle and land, and Holmes did not particularly like it, thinking the McSwains were marrying Chickasaw women so they could get more land. And I had hoped they would all get along. I never wanted to reveal my fears. I wiped my brow with my apron, and tried to bring my thoughts back to the present.

And then he asked me the question I had heard over and over that day. Mr. Murray asked me, "Is Holmes McLish ... he was your husband?"

I wiped my dry lips and answered once again, "Yes, sir."

The other commissioner cleared his throat. Mr. Murray pointed to him, and he asked me, "How far did you live from your daughter and this McSwain boy that lived with her at the time McLish was out here in the western part of the Chickasaw Nation?"

I told him I lived from one of the McSwain boys about eight miles, and about ten miles from the other. He nodded and Mr. Murray began again.

"When Holmes McLish was killed, were not he and the McSwain brothers, and all of you, all living in the same yard?" he asked.

I had hoped all this would be done with, but I was wrong. Mr.

Murray did not seem to waver when I told him, once again, that we were not living in the same yard, and that I was living eight miles away, at my home.

J.D.'s voice kept repeating in my head,

"Me brahther did nat mean to shoot 'im. Charley 'ard something, and thought it was a cattle rustler. Charley was shaht at in the dark! 'E just shaht back in self-defense! Thought it was one o' dahse damn cattle rustlers comin' through our prahperty."

I answered again, calm but firm, "I never lived with the McSwains. I had known my husband Holmes since I was eight years old. He was a good man, but he worked cattle out of Reck. That was his business and he owned holdings in that area as long as we were married."

The questioning went on repetitively regarding my sons-in-law. Over and over again Mr. Murray drove the nail into my heart, bruising my soul with questions that ripped all honor from me. He wanted to know if McSwain was ever at my house when Holmes was out in the western part of the Chickasaw Nation.

Ashamed, I went back to memories of my Holmes's face, holding him close. It was the only way I could keep my sanity through such insults. I blurted, after breathing deeply, as if I had lost some air, "The McSwain boys were not at my house! They had no business at my house!"

I told them all, again, that sometimes Holmes went to Reck for his cattle, and that the morning he was killed, I never saw him.

Holding back tears once more, I said, "He was gone a week out to Reck which is about how long it took him to go there. Holmes had some cattle stolen from him. Just after that we drew our annuity. I don't remember what exact day of the month it was. I gave him fifty-two dollars to get a man to help him get the cattle back."

I took a deep breath.

"Afterwards, he wrote to me that he'd located the man that stole the cattle," I finished with another sigh, "and that is the way the letter read."

"What happened after that?" the commissioner asked.

"He started home, I heard, and then he got to Joe Bynum's. I guess right there the men 'struck up' the whiskey. I never did find out who it was, or nothing about who had the cattle."

Mr. Murray left a few minutes and the other two whispered to each other. I reached in my pocket and felt the papers of integrity to make sure they were still there, in case someone asked for them.

Mr. Murray came back into the room with another paper. He asked me if Holmes McLish was married before he was married to me. I told him he was, and that I thought her name was Sis Dufer. He asked me if Holmes was married to any other woman before Sis Dufer. I told him Holmes was married to a white woman, but I did not know her name.

He pulled out the paper, laid it on the table, and asked, "Was her name Dorcas Moutray?"

I told Mr. Murray, "I don't know what her name was. Holmes was married four times before he married me. He also was married to Nancy Lewis."

"Did you ever have anything to do with these McSwain boys when your husband was off the western part of the Chickasaw Nation?"

I told him I didn't.

"Did you ever have anything to do with any other man?"

"No, sir," I replied with emphasis. I felt ashamed that they continued to ask me this question. I expected to be questioned, but I just did not want anyone to think such a thing of me. Here I am, with my boy. I want the best for him. How can they drag such awful things into it? Again, I wiped tears from my face. I flashed back to little Holmes's birth.

Ella and Belle were there with their husbands. Ella was my midwife. "Mama, you finally have a boy," I remembered Ella saying. "This was what you always wanted."

"Oh, Ella and Belle, and all my girls were all I ever wanted," I cried. "But this boy is so special."

I jolted back to reality. He asked me again where I was living when baby Holmes was born.

"I was living near Tishomingo," I said.

He asked, "Do you remember when they made the census in 1896?"

"I do, but I did not get the boy enrolled then. The man that did the enrollment did not enroll lots of people. I do not know why. He would come in and out of our yards at different times, and all my children were not all there at the same time. I think I was in Tishomingo with Holmes the day the census man came by," I answered as best I knew how.

A flash in time took me again to the day little Holmes was conceived. His father had come home from a long journey to Reck. He was so happy to see me. He told me how much he admired me all the years I struggled to raise my girls. He said I was a strong woman, pressed his lips to mine and told me how much he loved me.

I tried again to shake off my emotions.

The commissioner hammered at me again, "When they made up the 1896 census roll of the Chickasaw, why did they leave your boy off?

"I do not—I don't know why they left him off," I stammered. I told them I'd found out they had left him off just before I went to Colbert.

All the commissioners turned to each other again to whisper and the clerk stepped forward.

"Witness Esther McLish is excused."

His cold, raised voice startled me.

I quietly stood up and walked through the courthouse doors. I just kept walking. I did not look back. I wondered what the others that were being called in that day would say. I wondered what the commissioners thought of me now. They never asked for my letters of Christian and moral character. They still rested in my pocket. I touched them.

I knew my family would have been proud of me. Papa was there in spirit. He knew I stayed brave, braver than he would have ever imagined me to be. Ella waited by the courthouse steps, holding Holmes and Harry. I took Holmes and hugged him.

I gently turned his beautiful little face to mine. "You will be on the roll, Holmes!" I stated. "Just wait and see, my sweet boy. Just wait and see."

THE BIRTH OF HOLMES (1894)

September came quickly with the birth of my first and only son, Holmes Howard McLish, a handsome boy and popular with his five sisters. My grandson, Harry, also was proud to have another male child in the family.

But my family had been ripped apart by the horrible accident of the death of my husband Holmes. I knew Belle was just falling apart and I was getting quite worried about her. She was about ready to deliver their first baby, and so much wanting Charley to be there for her. And I worried about myself. I don't think I ever mourned my late husband. I rendered many prayers, and fell into a strange sort of sadness over it all. I feared someone was going to come in and take everything from us, as had happened to Mama and Papa during the Removal. I watched every day for the crows to come closer and start cawing at me. But they stayed on the fence by the corral.

Right after Holmes was killed, his brother, Richard, came to claim his body. He attended the funeral in Tishomingo, but not the wake the night before. I got a chance to visit with him after the funeral, but our talk was short, and he was not as friendly as he had been before, perhaps because of the awkwardness of the circumstances. I understood that Richard, being a lawyer and all, had to be cautious about talking with our family. And I reckoned there were many questions about the matter that were yet unanswered.

Articles appeared in the papers about Charley shooting Holmes. Charley was well-known in Denison, Texas, as a cattle rancher, so there were stories in that town's newspaper—some for him and some against. His sister, Minnie, was married to a prominent doctor there named Bailey and they were all upset about the publicity.

Richard turned out to play a strong part in bringing trial against Charley. He was a judge at the time, but stepped down because of his relationship to Holmes.

The trial was to start March 1, 1894, but was postponed until May. Belle and I at first believed the reason may have been because Charley was a white man married to an Indian woman. We soon learned we were right. A question had arisen as to who had jurisdiction of the case, between the federal government or the Chickasaw Nation.

The talk started rumbling in Tishomingo after it became an unusual dispute between the Chickasaw Nation and the United States court system. Some lawyers who represented the Chickasaw Nation, one I believed named Mr. Sandifer and another named Mr. C.H. Smith, claimed that the marriage of Charley McSwain to Belle Brown gave jurisdiction to the Chickasaw Nation's court.

Charley's lawyer, a Mr. A.B. Person, contended that United

States courts should hear the case. Belle told me that Mr. Sandifer and Mr. Person went down to meet in Paris, Texas, where it was decided that the Chickasaw Nation had jurisdiction. Charley would be tried in our Indian courts.

That did nothing to help with Belle's state of mind. She came to visit one afternoon, all worried about Charley.

"I am getting so tired of waiting," she cried. She had brought with her a copy of the Denison paper, with an article in it about the case and the matter of jurisdiction, told in heartless detail.

I took her hand. "Belle, we have to have patience. Remember in the Bible, Job taught us that we are to have patience," I reminded her. She leaned on me, her belly so big with baby. She looked like she was ready to explode. I worried about the stress on her, and on Charley, who spent his days in remorse.

She and Ella managed to post a bond to get him out of jail in time to see the birth of his little girl, Maud.

My holidays passed mostly without Ella and Belle, although they came when they could. Ella was especially diligent to allow me to be a part of her family, even after she became pregnant again the following year. She would name her new daughter Minnie, after Charley's sister. Girls just seemed to run in the family. And little Maud was a comfort to Belle, although she wanted to wait to have more children, until they knew what would happen to Charley. Shortly after that decision, Belle found out she was pregnant again.

I dreamed about Holmes's death often. I think I was letting my mind create ways to mourn him. It seemed unfair that I never got to cry much over losing him. But I did see his handsome face every day, in his son, who looked just like him.

As I came to terms with what I knew about Holmes's drinking problem, which he had for long before we were married, I realized that was probably why his first couple of wives left him. I found out more about it after we were married, although he kept it under control around me. He knew I was a religious woman, and that I would not like him coming home drunk, which he never did the entire time we were seeing each other. Even after we were married, he never showed me at any time that he would partake in that "spirit" drink. I was thankful for that.

Nevertheless, I would hear talk in town that he had been drinking when he left Joe Bynum's place for home the night he died. Talk was free in our town, and there was a lot of it. I did not accept it all as true, because there was never a time that he came home to me drunk. Still, my doubts would not go away.

Ella stopped by soon after she and Belle posted bond for Charley.

"We got the bond all posted, Mama. I am glad that Charley will be home with his new baby," she said, kind of simply.

I could tell she really needed to visit with me. "That's good news, Ella," I said, "But it seems you have more to talk about today than that."

She sighed, then nodded. "Why do you think Holmes came in the middle of the night to Charley's and Belle's place, Mama?"

"I don't know. I am just not sure of any of this, at all," I said. "Only Holmes could tell us, and he is gone."

"I know it was very dark, Mama, and he could not see anything. The witnesses said he fired two shots before Charley shot back. That's what I just can't make any sense of!"

"But poor Holmes was shot in the back, Ella," I pointed out. "Maybe he realized he was lost, and he'd turned to head home."

"I am so confused about all this." She sat with me, almost sobbing.

"Oh, Ella, he loved you, dear, and he wanted to return those cows to me. He spoke so highly about the time when you helped him with that calf. You remember?"

"I do, Mama." She wiped her face with my apron.

I tried to help her find comfort and understanding. "When we talked, before he left for Reck, I reminded him that those cows were given to you by Lottie's husband, Nathan, after she'd died. Holmes felt like he needed to get those cows back because of you, Ella. I know that for sure."

"I know how people talk in town, Mama," she said. "And I also know that it would not have been any of the McSwains stealing your cows. We have all the cows we would ever need."

"Oh, you need to just ignore that talk. Didn't you tell me that some of the McSwains' cattle were stolen just recently?"

She dried up at that. "Yes. We've been on the alert for rustlers, just like everyone else."

"Holmes may have been going by there to tell you he found our cows, and saw someone trespass on your place, and shot at them, and then turned to come home," I said.

"I hope they find out the truth, and Charley is set free," she smiled and kissed my cheek.

"I have to go now, Mama, but I will come back and spend more time with you."

I watched her ride away on her horse, longing for more time with her, but thankful for the visit. I went into deeper thoughts about Holmes's death after she left. I did not want to think anything ill of any of my husbands or any of my children, and I knew time would bring us the answers soon. But I also knew, deep inside, that the spirits of that drink created such problems for those who indulged. I hoped Holmes had not been drinking. Most men could not think clearly, I believed, with those spirits in them. I also knew in my heart that Charley never meant to kill him.

Charley went to trial the following year before a special judge named Joe Maytubby. Late on a Saturday evening, the jury announced that they had arrived at a verdict, and were dismissed with instructions to appear the following Monday to give it. However, in the meantime, a heavy rain fell, and all the creeks rose around Tishomingo. Only part of the jury showed up on Monday, the rest being unable to make it to court because of the high waters. On that Wednesday, a full quorum arrived, and announced a verdict of guilty of first-degree murder. A motion for a new trial was made.

In November 1899, Judge Maytubby granted a new trial for the next September, agreeing with Charley's lawyer about the irregularities with the jury because of the floods in Tishomingo. Again, Belle was granted bond to take Charley home.

The following year, Charley's sister Minnie got a divorce from Dr. Bailey, which affected Charley, because he had always felt responsible for the talk in Denison about him going to trial for murder. He was sure he'd messed up his sister's marriage. I tried to persuade him not to take blame for things he did not know everything about, especially concerning Holmes. I shared my theory that Holmes might have followed some cattle rustlers to Charley's place and took some shots at them.

I prayed to God to forgive him and prayed he would forgive himself. I hoped the courts would do the same.

He would always hug me and tell me, "Thanks, Nana." I realized our family had become closer because of that horrible accident. Little Holmes, now five years old, and I began to stay often with Ella and her husband. J.D. had lost an arm in a wagon accident right after my husband's death and could not do a lot of the hard work around his place. That meant Charley worked both places with a few hired hands. Money seemed to never be an issue with the McSwain boys and they were both devoted to their wives.

Belle gave birth to Willie, Joel Dayton, and Luella during the time they awaited a final trial that might send Charley to prison. He hated going anywhere in Tishomingo, where he was always watched or questioned by someone. "When is the trial, Charley?" some would ask. He even received threatening letters. Now and then, a stone was thrown at their porch. I worried about Belle, but she stood beside Charley with all the love that a woman could give to a man. Her grandpa would have been proud of her.

THE INTERVIEW OF LAVINA KING

Late in the afternoon of March 28, 1904, a letter came from Lavina, our sweet Nana, bearing a description of her interview with the commission. I pressed it against my heart a few moments, thinking of the past and that it was a message from the mother of my first love, Benjamin.

Oh, my dear, sweet Benjamin, I thought. He was such a unique and wonderful man. My love for him had been as close to perfection as anyone could ever imagine.

The letter I held was from a woman who had helped journey me into womanhood, and I hoped it would tell me something that would help me to know that, after all my days of labor and hard work, my little Holmes would be registered, and get his Chickasaw roll number.

I pulled a newly quilted blanket lightly across and over my tired, old legs. I had worked out in the field earlier in the day and had come inside to prepare some bread for my grandchildren, who were sure to stop by in the next hour or so.

I opened the letter.

My dearest Little Bird,

I met with the commission for the Five Civilized Tribes on the 21st of March 1904. The first thing they asked me was my name. I stated it was Lavina King, since that is my married name, now.

They asked my age, and I told them I was seventy-one or so. I could not remember exactly. They continued with many questions about how long I lived in the Choctaw Nation, and asked if I was a citizen on the roll and I told them, of course, I was.

They wanted to know how long I had known you, and I told them since you were twelve years old. That is a long time, my dear Little Bird. Then I wanted to laugh because they asked me if you were a white woman. I thought to myself, well, my goodness gentleman, are you blind? But of course, I did not say that. Calm down, Little Bird.

I told them you were Cherokee and Choctaw, and that you were born and raised in Indian Territory. They went on to ask if Benjamin Frazier was my son, and was he married to you? I told them he was, that Benjamin was Chickasaw by birth, and you were his wife.

They wanted to know about your wedding and if I was at it. I am not sure why they think people get married these days without family present, but I guess some do. You know that we were raised better. I told them I was there, and Judge Jegle married you two, and the ceremony was beautiful. You actually jumped over a broom afterwards, but I did not share that funny moment with them. They continued to want to know if you were married by a District Judge, and I told them he was.

I kept worrying about what they were going to ask me, but the questions were easy and simple. They wanted to know where you all lived after you two were married, and I told them on the Blue River about two miles from us. I told them you all were married almost three years before my Benjamin died. I told them about the wagon accident on the Blue. It was hard, Little Bird, to tell them that story, but I knew I must, for your little baby's sake. They wanted to know if there was any separation or divorce during this time, and I thought to myself, if they only knew how much you loved my son. Again, they asked me if Benjamin was Choctaw by blood, and it seemed all I kept saying was, "yes, sir," over and over again.

Then they asked me who you were married to after Benjamin and I told them Houston Brown and that he was full-blood Chickasaw. They asked me if Houston was alive today, and I told them, "no." I told them that he died when my granddaughters were six and four. Then I explained I was living with you and Houston after my husband, Dixon, died and I consider your children with Houston my grandchildren, as well. They wanted to know if Houston Brown was married previously before you and I told them I did not think he was married, that I know of, to anyone before his marriage to you.

Then he wanted to know how soon you married Houston Brown after Benjamin's death. I told them it was a little over a year. I then was asked how long you were married to Houston and I told them seven years, before he was killed. Then they asked me about Jim Wolf, and if I knew that you were married to Jim, and I said yes, and that you two were married in the Chickasaw Nation.

I am sending you an actual copy of the transcript.

All my love,
Nana

I remembered seeing her sitting outside the council of the Five Civilized Tribes the day Ella and I traveled to Muskogee. I knew she had been asked to speak on my behalf and we embraced. Ella considered her a grandmother and Lavina was so glad to see her all grown up. She sat on the bench outside with us and I enjoyed our time together before she was called into the room to testify.

She had kept her promise, to divulge in a letter what was said in her interview. I know she hoped her interview would help me to get my little boy on the Dawes roll. I cried over it, as if it was only yesterday when I lost Benjamin. I think my bravery truly commenced the day I lost him.

I laid the letter and transcript down on the table and looked at the floor in front of me, as blank and brown as my skin. I felt seized by an implacable fear that I was never going to see my last child get his rightful land that he so deserved. My whole life's work and effort rested in the hands of five men who did not even know me or understand my Indian heritage. They did not look at me as person, as I told my story and the truth with all my heart. They looked at me by my skin color, and I awaited to be numbered by them. I clasped my hands together and rendered a prayer that God would give me the grace to handle my fears.

"Be brave, Little Bird," came a soft whisper from the past, to lay on my mind.

THE FALA DEPART

In January 1903 came a bad winter storm, during which Belle sent word by one of their hired hands to ask me to come to her settlement right away. I wasn't sure I could get the wagon down the road, what with icy patches here and there. So, the man Belle sent drove little Holmes and me in our wagon. Hattie had married James "Andy" Orr, and Mattie and Francis were at boarding school. It was freezing cold, but the man told me Belle's request was urgent.

I walked into her house to find her sobbing in a room full of people. I recognized the sheriff from Tishomingo, his deputy, and a constable from the Chickasaw Nation whose name I did not know. I ran past them toward my Belle.

Then I saw blood all over the floor and Charley's body, limp in a chair next to the window. Someone had covered the top of his head with a handkerchief, blood soaked through it from the right side of his face next to the window where he sat. I saw a great hole in the window pane. It looked like a bullet had passed through. I turned little Holmes's head away from the sight, and took him and Belle to the back hallway.

"Oh, Mama, my Charley is dead," she cried in my arms. Her face was swollen from crying, her dress and hands covered in his blood.

"Let's go to the bedroom." I walked her that way, keeping Holmes close and his eyes away from the traumatic scene before us. To this day, I still see his head covered with that awful, bloody cloth.

The sheriff stopped me, wanting to talk. Belle clutched my arm, crying uncontrollably. "Sheriff, please let me get my child and daughter out of this room," I said to him. He nodded. I took her into the bedroom to sit, and told her to wait a few minutes, that I would be right back.

The sheriff stayed close, as if afraid I might run off somewhere.

"Mrs. McLish, we were summoned by a hired hand. I arrived and found Mrs. McSwain covered in blood. She told me that not long after she put the children to bed, she heard her husband emit a loud scream that no man should make, and came running out of the bedroom. She found Mr. McSwain bleeding from his head in the chair. I think she must have tried to stop the bleeding." He took a breath. "She was very lucky that she wasn't shot, as well."

I looked at all the people standing around the room. And then there was Charley, there in his chair with a newspaper, covered in the bloodied cloth by the window. It all looked like a very bad dream.

The sheriff continued, "Apparently, an unknown man slipped up and shot Mr. McSwain, clean through the window. I am not a doctor, but it appears the bullet shattered poor Mr. McSwain's jaw. He was bleeding immensely by the time Mrs. McSwain got to him."

He paused, crossing his arms over his chest like a man of authority. "I am afraid when you get shot in the face like that, there isn't much that can be done. I am sure he bled to death before Mrs. McSwain could get help," he said.

My only wish was to run out of the room and back to Belle. I took a deep breath and pointed at Charley.

"So, he bled to death from the shot through his jaw?"

The sheriff nodded. "She said the whole side of his face was gone." He walked over to Charley and lifted the cloth.

I almost lost everything inside me. I turned away, covering my mouth to keep from being sick.

He stopped me again. "Mrs. McLish, let me finish." He looked a bit angry at me for wanting to leave the room.

"I am sorry, sheriff." I apologized and found a chair to sit.

He told me one of the hired hands caught a man sneaking behind the corral and Charley died a few minutes after that. Still, the sheriff said he was "happy" to report to me that they did catch the man who shot Charley. I did not care for his choice of words and thought I was going to be sick again. He assured me that one of his deputies had already taken the man off to jail in Tishomingo.

I thanked the sheriff and went back toward the bedroom, realizing with surprise that Belle's children were not awakened by the commotions. I opened their bedroom door, ever so slightly, to see all were still sleeping.

Holmes, drowsy and whimpering, came to me. I told him to lay down on his big sister's bed and Mama would be beside him, real soon. I ached for him, having left him sitting with Belle in this room, and her in a trance, covered with blood. It was a horrible scene that no child should have to see.

"Oh, my darling Belle, I am back now. Let your Mama clean you up," I cleaned blood from my daughter's face. "Turn away, child. Don't look at your hands." I tried my best to keep my supper inside. Holmes drifted off on the bed. I am not sure he was ever fully awake enough to be aware of what went on.

I got Belle a change of clothes and left her to put them on. I went to check on her children again. They were all still sound asleep. I am not sure how, but the Lord was protecting them that night. I rendered a quick prayer at their doorway and asked the deputy to keep an eye on their rooms because I did not want them to come out and see their father. I hoped they would take his body away soon.

I asked the sheriff about that. "The coroner is on his way, Mrs. McLish. As soon as he gets here and pronounces Mr. McSwain dead, and that it was a murder, then they will take his body to town to prepare him for burial."

"I will go and get a quilt to lay over the body until the doctor arrives," I said. I found an old one in the closet and I took it to the deputy, who laid it on Charley, and returned to sit quietly in the hallway. I made Belle stay with Holmes in her bedroom until Charley was removed.

It took about another hour for all the work to be done. Belle lay down next to little Holmes and cried herself to sleep. I took a bucket out to the barrel by the side of the house and got rainwater to clean the blood off the floor. The chair Charley had sat in was covered with it and I asked the deputy to carry it out to the barn.

The sun began to rise while I finished cleaning. I was exhausted, but kept myself busy, and rendered a prayer that we would be spared from anything more. It was too much for me to handle. But I did.

Proving innocence or guilt was becoming a topic of conversation in our family. No one ever knew why this man shot Charley. I never knew why Holmes fired into Charley's yard, or why Charley fired back. I only knew that sometimes, when money and cattle and whiskey get in the way of a man's thinking, things turn away from the truth. I prayed every day after the loss of my husband Holmes. We had so little time together, but I saw his eyes in our son. I could only pray for Belle like I had never prayed before, and hoped she would get her life in order. Her loss was great, but she knew Charley loved her deeply.

No one should lose loved ones like we did.

I did not want my daughter trapped in a life of endless sorrow and longing for her husband. I did not want my children to live a life without a vision for their future. I had to help them to begin again, as I did. I hoped my daughters would follow the same dream I had for a better life.

The day after Charley's death, I watched the three crows fly off, as if their services were no longer required. As if leaving us permanently.

What are those crows doing?

Did they think I would no longer need them to warn us of danger? Or were they just bearers of death? I wanted to throw something at them. Their black wings shone in the morning light, and they lifted their heads to the east. I will never know for certain why they always appeared for me. I hoped no more fala would come to visit. Papa told me they were important, these "truth-talkers," but this Indian woman had experienced all the truth she could ever want in one lifetime.

A NEW BEGINNING (1904)

I received a letter on September 8, 1904, from Tams Bixby and the law firm of Thompson and Brown, telling me I had been rendered a citizen of the Chickasaw Nation by intermarriage.

I was enrolled. I could hardly believe it. I was getting a Chickasaw roll number, as one who had been married to four Chickasaw men. But months would pass without hearing anything more. I had written my attorney and the commission. I waited again for someone's decision about my life.

Winter folded into spring. We fought a tornado that barely missed our home in late May. Our neighbor to the west lost their barn, but our place just had lots of tree limbs down. It was not until June of 1905, I received a letter of affirmation that my son Holmes was approved and enrolled as a citizen of the Chickasaw Nation.

It was a bittersweet victory. So much had happened to get me to this day. I thought about my journey in life, from that quiet ride one early morning on Thunder to at last realizing a place in the world of Indian Territory. I was not in any way different from any other Indian girl. My parents cared about the world they lived in. My Papa and Mama had been strong in faith. My brother and sister had helped me grow up to be brave.

The journey my children took to follow me as I moved from one event to the next made for quite a story. They were blessed by a heritage of tribal histories, from Cherokee and Choctaw, to Chickasaw. I was a mother who understood the journey her parents took during Indian Removal, and each of my children had Chickasaw fathers whose parents also came in the Removal. That heritage gave us strength to share with our children and our children's children.

My life was a journey that others had made alongside me, and I knew their stories were not greater or lesser than mine. My family were settlers of Indian Territory. We became farmers and ranchers, constables and lawmakers, storekeepers, mothers and fathers. We raised some of the finest horses and cattle on the grasslands of our territory.

We planted great crops, and our cotton and our corn were known as superior. Travelers came by train to learn from us. Missionaries helped us to establish our schools. We recovered from the pain of death and murder, the loss of life and loved ones. We wrote rules and constitutions and bills. We cleared forests and built towns, but mostly, we loved. I had loved more than anyone could ever have imagined.

On that day, I began to teach my son Holmes to be a better horseback rider. He had a new horse named Spirit that his big sister Ella had trained, and we rode to the Washita River together. I wanted to teach him the way my Papa taught me, to get out and smell and feel the wind, to touch the earth and smell the flowers.

"Mama, why do you love horses so much?" Holmes asked.

Holmes had a calm nature about him and he had become my tallest child, slender and very handsome. He wanted to learn about everything. I was happy to be his teacher.

"Well, my son, horses are spirits with souls. They take us safely where we want to go and they travel on God's wings," I said. I saw he was ready to run Spirit.

"Is that why Ella named my horse Spirit?"

"Yes, Holmes. He is your horse, to take you safely wherever you want to go. Just always be kind to him. Remember to be gentle. He is sensitive, and can feel just the least little movement you make," I instructed. "Your horse can even feel the touch of a feather."

"How can a horse feel the touch of a feather? He's a big animal, and he clomps his feet. He could not feel a feather at all, could he?"

"Let me show you, son." I slid down. "Get down off your horse." I reached for the rope to hold his horse, a rope I had made for him.

"Point your finger straight, like an arrow," I told him. "Now, move it slowly, straight towards Spirit's side, but when you get to his fur, just gently touch it with the tip of your finger, like the touch a feather would make."

He did, and saw Spirit's skin shudder ever so slightly.

"Wow, Mama. Did you see Spirit's skin move?"

"I did, son. A horse can feel your slightest touch," I continued. "That's how a horse flicks a fly off his skin. Spirit is sensitive to every movement. He is wild like the wind, but calm and sensitive, like a feather," I explained.

Holmes smiled and reached his arms around Spirit's neck to give him a hug.

"Always know you are Chickasaw, my son," I said with love in my heart. "Always know our skin is soft and sensitive, but also know inside our Indian skin, we are brave and tough." I smiled and handed the rope back to him. "Your bravery will take you far, like your horse Spirit will take you far," I continued, taking on my papa's way of telling a story. "Your horse will weave you through life, like the cord on this rope. Your rope will give you many changes. Sometimes it will give you happiness, and sometimes it will make you sad. Sometimes it will pull you tight, and sometimes it will just let you go. You must always keep your rope close to you, and be brave."

"I will, Mama. I am Chickasaw, I will be brave," Holmes replied, holding the rope. "Chikasha saya," he said, affirming he was Chickasaw. Then he added, "Fala ishto saya," meaning "I am Raven."

I was struck. "Where did you get that name, son?"

"That is what my friends call me, the Raven," he said. "I am the brave truth-talker."

I rendered a prayer of thanksgiving to God.

I saw again the three crows taking flight that day, lightly swooping before me and my horse to follow my son, Raven. We rode along the banks of the Washita River, on a journey into our new beginning.

AUTHOR'S NOTE

I came to the full realization of my own history after seven years of genealogical research. I had created a family tree online, adding link after link of documents, and had come across the actual transcripts of council meetings Esther, my great-great-grandmother, had with the Dawes Commission. Through my research, I saw how our tribal leaders' powers were restricted, the United States government placed multitudes of families on reservations, or forced them to begin life anew in a strange land, while the rest of the nation turned a blind eye. First American families had to make it or break it. It suddenly became very personal to me and I just sat down and cried. I was so driven to tell the story of my great-great-grandmother, Esther McLish—a story of struggle, love, and courage. But beyond that was the story of a woman with a vision, passed down to her from her father, and a determination to make that vision a reality.

The following pages are a few examples of letters, roll cards, and article excerpts I found during my research, and pertain to the real-life individuals on which the characters of this book are based. I hope these mementos serve as a revelation of the very real heartache and perseverance many First Americans experienced during this era.

May we all find strength in the stories of our ancestors.

ESTHER'S FAMILY TREE

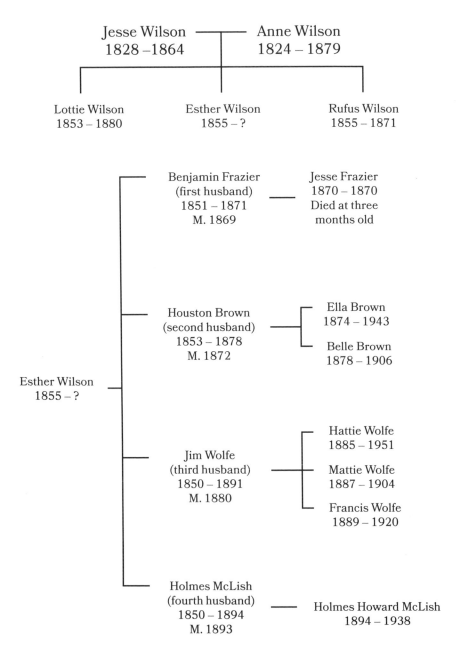

Jesse Wilson
1828 – 1864
——
Anne Wilson
1824 – 1879

Lottie Wilson
1853 – 1880

Esther Wilson
1855 – ?

Rufus Wilson
1855 – 1871

Esther Wilson
1855 – ?

Benjamin Frazier
(first husband)
1851 – 1871
M. 1869
——
Jesse Frazier
1870 – 1870
Died at three
months old

Houston Brown
(second husband)
1853 – 1878
M. 1872
Ella Brown
1874 – 1943

Belle Brown
1878 – 1906

Jim Wolfe
(third husband)
1850 – 1891
M. 1880
Hattie Wolfe
1885 – 1951

Mattie Wolfe
1887 – 1904

Francis Wolfe
1889 – 1920

Holmes McLish
(fourth husband)
1850 – 1894
M. 1893
——
Holmes Howard McLish
1894 – 1938

THE FAMILY TREE BRANCH OF
MARY RUTH SCOTT BARNES

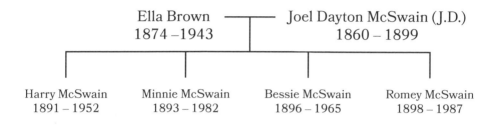

| Ella Brown | | Joel Dayton McSwain (J.D.) |
| 1874 – 1943 | | 1860 – 1899 |

| Harry McSwain | Minnie McSwain | Bessie McSwain | Romey McSwain |
| 1891 – 1952 | 1893 – 1982 | 1896 – 1965 | 1898 – 1987 |

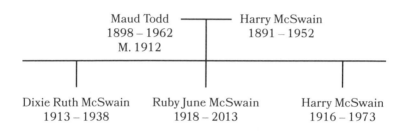

Maud Todd		Harry McSwain
1898 – 1962		1891 – 1952
M. 1912		

| Dixie Ruth McSwain | Ruby June McSwain | Harry McSwain |
| 1913 – 1938 | 1918 – 2013 | 1916 – 1973 |

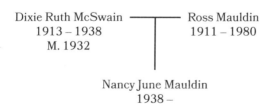

Dixie Ruth McSwain		Ross Mauldin
1913 – 1938		1911 – 1980
M. 1932		

Nancy June Mauldin
1938 –

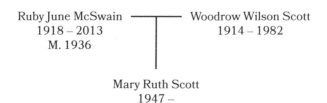

Ruby June McSwain		Woodrow Wilson Scott
1918 – 2013		1914 – 1982
M. 1936		

Mary Ruth Scott
1947 –

Submitted by and with the permission of Rosemary Holderman, the great-great-granddaughter of Lottie Wilson. Rosemary was very helpful throughout my research and offered this wonderful statement, shared with her by her great-uncle.

In an interview with JB Kendall on June 13, 2000.
Byars, Oklahoma

Mr. Kendall said,

"Lottie Wilson was married to William Nathan Price after the death of Mama's father Tuskatubby. Mr. Price owned thousands of acres of land south of Byars, Oklahoma. He came from Mississippi.

"The family Bible has an old newspaper article from the McAlester paper. It is about an Indian with the last name of Wolf and about a murder. JB has often wondered if there is some connection to the family that motivated Mama to keep this article. Mama's great aunt Esther Wilson (Lottie's sister) married a man named Wolf. Esther's daughter married a McSwain, and she thinks Esther lived to be very old. Papa Finley claimed he saw Esther riding her horse in Ada, Oklahoma when she was 115. She married several times."

Dawes Roll Card of Esther McLish, circa 1904.

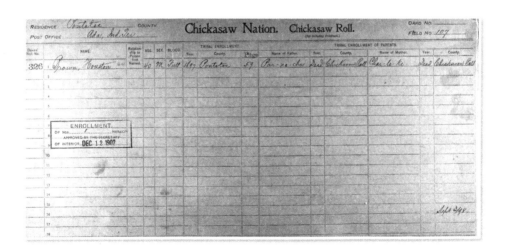

Dawes Roll Card of Houston Brown, circa 1902.

Tishomingo County
Chickasaw Nation
May 24th 1893

In accordance with the ordances of the M. E Church South and being an ordained Local preacher, being vested with the right to solmenize Marriages do this day join togather in the Holy bonds of Matrimony Holmes. Mc Lish and Mrs Hester Wolf

C. A Burris

Recorded May. 26th 1893

A. T. Mc Kinney
Clerk Ts - C.N.

I. T.S Harris. County & Probate Clerk. of Tishoming County do say. that the above is a true and correct coppy of the original this certifyed to the 23rd of December 1902

T.S Harris
Clerk T.C.C.N.

Record of marriage between Esther Wolf and Holmes Mclish, circa 1893.

HOLMES M'LISH KILLED.

News was received today that Holmes McLish, brother of Richard McLish, of this city, was shot and instantly killed at Tishomingo yesterday by a man named McSwain, a brother of one-armed McSwain, well known in Ardmore.

McLish was shot twice in the back, and strange as it may seem, McSwain claims it was accidental.

None of the minute particulars could be obtained, and in their absence the 'Ardmoreite refrains from expressing an opinion. It is the general belief, however, that it was murder most foul.

Richard McLish has gone to the scene of the killing to take charge of the remains of his deceased brother.

Newspaper clipping of Holmes McLish's death from *The Daily Ardmoreite*, February 28, 1894, Vol. I, No. 103.

MURDER AT TISHOMINGO

Chas. McSwain Killed by an Unknown Negro.

Tishmingo, I. T., Jan. 25.—Chas. McSwain, a brother of Dick McSwain, who was killed by one John Edwards at Durwood some time ago, was shot here yesterday by a negro whose name could not be learned.

The negro slipped up to the window of a brightly lighted room in which McSwain was sitting, and shot him through the window.

The bullet shattered his jawbone, inflicting an extremely painful if not serious wound. The negro has been arrested.

Newspaper clipping of Charley McSwain's murder from *The Daily Times-Journal*, January, 25, 1901, Vol. 12, No. 221.

219

An Interesting Case.

DENISON, Tex., Mar. 16.—Governor Wolf of the Cnickasaw nation yesterday issued a requisition on Governor Hogg for the person of Charles McSwain, who is now in Sherman before the commissioners' court, to answer for the killing of a man named Holmes McLish, near Tishomingo, several weeks ago. The requisition is in charge of Constable McGill of the Tishomingo district, who was in Denison to-day en route for his prisoner.

At the time of the killing a dispute arose between the Indian and government officers as to what court should try the case. A little over two years ago all the whites in the Chickasaw nation were disfranchised—debarred from holding office, voting or taking any part in the affairs of the nation, and upon that law the government officers claimed and took the prisoner. On the other hand, McSwain married an Indian, holds lands, but has nothing to do with government affairs. That he is still a citizen of the Chickasaw nation is the stand the nation takes, hence the requisition. This is the first time on record that such a process has been issued by the Indian government, and the outcome will be watched with interest by friends of both factions.

Newspaper report of the requisition of Charley McSwain, shortly after the death of Holmes McLish from *The Indian Journal*, March 22, 1894, Vol. XVIII, No. 15.

SHOT AND KILLED.

Intelligence was recieved in the city to-day of a fatal tragedy which occured last Saturday on the Sandy in Tishomingo county, Chickasaw Nation. Charley McSwain shot and Holmes McLish, a Chickasaw Indian Charley McSwain is wellknown in Denison, having resided here.

Later—A letter received in this city this afternoon gives the following particulars reguarding the killing.

McSwain and McLish had had some previous difficulty. They met and McLish fired at McSwain twice, when McSwain returned the fire killing him. McSwain surrendered to the officers and was released on a $500 bond. The deceased is a cousin of the Hon. Richard McLish, Superintendent of education, Chickasaw nation. The dead man is about twenty-three years of age.—Denison Herald.

Another report of Holmes McLish's death from
The Caddo Banner, March 2, 1894, Vol. 4, No. 9.

Chas. McSwain, convicted of the murder of Holmes McLish, has been granted a new trial by Special Judge Maytubby. The irregularities on the part of the jury furnished ground for the ruling of the court. Some of the best legal talent in Ardmore will be employed in the case for the next trial.

News of Charley McSwain's new trial date from *The Daily Ardmoreite*,
November 26, 1899, Vol. 7, No. 24.

LITTLE

BIRD